CARNY KNOWLEDGE

Trapped in the body of a 1950s carnival worker, Sam Beckett learns the true meaning of thrills and chills. According to Al, Sam's holographic contact with the future, a roller coaster will derail in four days . . .

The accident will result in seven deaths . . .

And Sam's chances of stopping it are—one in a million.

QUANTUM LEAP
THE NOVEL

QUANTUM LEAP

A NOVEL BY
ASHLEY McCONNELL
BASED ON THE UNIVERSAL TELEVISION
SERIES "QUANTUM LEAP"
CREATED BY DONALD P. BELLISARIO

ACE BOOKS, NEW YORK

Quantum Leap, a novel by Ashley McConnell, based on the Universal television series QUANTUM LEAP, created by Donald P. Bellisario.

This book is an Ace original edition, and has never been previously published.

QUANTUM LEAP

An Ace Book / published by arrangement with
MCA Publishing Rights, a Division of MCA, Inc.

PRINTING HISTORY
Ace edition / November 1992

ISBN: 0–441–69322–9

Ace Books are published by The Berkley Publishing Group,
200 Madison Avenue, New York, New York 10016.
The name "ACE" and the "A" logo are trademarks
belonging to Charter Communications, Inc.

PRINTED IN THE UNITED STATES OF AMERICA

10 9 8 7 6 5 4 3 2 1

ACKNOWLEDGMENTS

No book comes out of nowhere, especially this one. The author gratefully acknowledges Ginjer Buchanan's excellent memory, Nancy Holder's assertiveness lessons and brainstorming in time of need, and Kathryn Ptacek's critical eye. In addition, Gary Hays of Cliff's Familyland provided a wealth of essential information about amusement parks and what really *can't* go wrong with roller coasters (any errors on this topic are strictly my own).

And, of course, Don P. Bellisario, Deborah Pratt, Scott Bakula and Dean Stockwell, and all the others at Bellisarius Productions, without whom there would be no Quantum Leap.

QUANTUM LEAP

PROLOGUE

He was floating somewhere, lost in blue-white light, waiting for the voice, the anchor, the thread back to reality that would tell him he was not absolutely alone.

There was no sensation, no weight, scent, taste, nothing but the light surrounding him. He might have been moving; he could not tell. He had no body. If he was moving, through air, through space, through electronic circuits, there was no way to tell. If time was passing, in either direction, there was no way to tell.

"Dr. Beckett."

There it was! The voice for which he had been waiting.

It surrounded him as the light surrounded him, was a part of himself as the light was a

1

part of himself, was himself.

"Yes." He made words without lips and teeth and tongue to form them, thought words and heard them as he heard the voice, without ears. If he had had a body, he might have looked about him, searching for the source of the voice, for someone to whom to give the answer, "Here I am."

It was important that the voice know he was there. That someone know he was there. That someone find him.

He had the sensation of being examined, of an intellectual curiosity, as if it were his turn to be the specimen under the microscope, subjected to examination and experimentation.

"Are you ready, Dr. Beckett?" the voice said. But it did not wait for an answer. It had never once waited for an answer. His willingness, his readiness was a matter of indifference, as the willingness of the worm to be dissected was a matter of indifference to the student. At last, there was the sensation of movement, of rushing through great consequences, of being tossed and torn by something for which he had no name, of being carried to a destination he had not chosen.

"Am I going home?" he cried out, and knew there was enough of himself—whatever he was—present to feel the wailings of despair. He could not remember "home." All he knew was that it was a good place, his place, where he had an identity and friends and people knew

who he was, where he knew other people, and he wanted desperately to be there. Home was some other place than this blue light.

Miraculously, the sensation of rushing through canyons stopped, as if the experimenter had paused between the dissecting table and the electron microscope to look once again at the stained slide it carried. "Home! Oh no, you're not going home yet. You're not ready, not yet.

"But soon. Very soon. I promise."

July 10, 1957
Wednesday

CHAPTER ONE

"Bob, you're doing it again." A woman's voice, filled with infinite scorn. Or, possibly worse, compassion. He was trying too hard to catch his balance to be sure, and the voice was softened with an unfamiliar drawl. Things were still blurry, but there was an impression of bright lights in darkness, the smell of—popcorn?, the feel of a woman's arm under his hand, and—

His vision sharpened, focused on the woman and then, shockingly, on the sandy-haired man behind her, aiming the rifle at—him?—her?

He yanked the woman toward him and down, twisting himself over her, knowing that there was no way mortal flesh could beat a bullet but knowing he had to *try*, ignoring her shriek. His back hit something that wobbled, creaked, and he tucked her head into the curve of his arm and

7

squeezed his eyes tight, waiting for the shot.

The woman didn't appreciate the rescue. She was yelling at him, beating at him with her free hand.

The barrier creaked again and collapsed on his head, hard but not, fortunately, too heavy.

There was no shot.

He opened one eye to see a two-dimensional yellow duck dangling from a pulley, and a well-manicured fist descending with purpose toward his face. He ducked, and heard a ladylike oath.

He began to suspect that all was not as it appeared. "Oh boy," he muttered resignedly.

It was going to be one of those Leaps.

Sam Beckett noted with relief that at least he was a man this time—he could tell by the shoes. That was a little comfort, anyway. He staggered to his feet, shoving plywood out of the way, and offered his hand to the woman in the wreckage.

"Look, I'm really sorry," he began.

"Sorry!" The woman was speechless with fury. At least it gave him a chance to help her up and brush ineffectually at the splinters on her clothes. She was in her mid-twenties, with plaster-pattered black hair cut in a shoulder-length flip style, and she was dressed in a long narrow skirt and a once-white blouse, and wearing nylons and spike heels. She was rubbing gingerly at her eye.

Sam was distracted from his appreciation.

"Hey, don't do that, you could damage the cornea."

A man's laughter, as she slapped his hand away, reminded him of the guy with the rifle. He spun around.

The man put the gun down on the bench separating them, stuck his hands in his pockets, and was laughing heartily. "Oh, boy, if you could have *seen* yourself! You looked like you thought I was really going to shoot you!" Almost as an afterthought, he added, "Miss Aline, are you okay?"

"Oh, I'm just fine." Aline—the woman whose life he had tried to save—stepped out of the wreckage, kicking the yellow duck out of the way with one pointed toe, and glared at him. One eye was definitely bloodshot.

"Now blast it, Bob, I asked you to handle the game, not pull it down around my ears!" The quivering in her voice might have been tears. It probably wasn't, he decided. She looked too mad. She brushed her hands together and winced as another splinter announced itself. "What's this nonsense about metal bolts?"

He didn't even try to answer that one.

So his name was Bob this time. Well, it was a start. And her name was Aline. Now if he could find out the name of the jerk with the gun, he'd be way ahead.

His right hip ached, probably from hitting the back of the open booth. Glancing around, he saw a line of ducks tilted at a mechanically incorrect angle. It was one of those games where you shot at the ducks and knocked them over and won a prize. He should have won the big one, then; the ducks were in the dust, and most of the stuffed animals hanging from the canvas roof were too. His reflexes had brought down almost the whole flimsy structure. All that was left was the front counter and part of one wall. One particularly garish green monkey had buffered his back from the impact of the support post. He set it on its rump with a grateful pat.

A little girl peering over the bench took a finger out of the corner of her mouth long enough to announce, "That's not Bob." Announcement made, the finger went right back in her mouth.

Out of the mouths of babes, as Al would say, though he usually wasn't referring to babes this small. About four, he judged. And she had to be standing on something in order to look over the counter. She had huge blue eyes and white-blonde hair and a dirty nose.

"Bessa, go home," Aline ordered. "It's past your bedtime."

Bessa hopped down from whatever she'd been standing on and disappeared.

"Listen, I'm sorry, I thought—"

"You're always sorry, Bob. Look, get this mess cleaned up, okay. See if you can get it working." She looked at the line of ducks on the floor, sighed. "On second thought, just get it cleaned up."

The sandy-haired man on the other side

laughed again, opened a flap in the counter, and bowed Aline out of the booth. "I'll be back to check it out in case you do get it working again," he called back over his shoulder.

"Bob" watched them go, noticing that who-ever the sandy-haired man was, he didn't put his arm around Aline. Out of such small victories, comfort was made.

He looked around, trying to find himself. The smell of popcorn and the bright lights made sense now; he was standing in the midway of a carnival of some kind. It was summertime, sweltering hot, and the western sky held the remains of sunset. An almost-full moon was getting brighter as the sky darkened.

A few teenagers sauntered between the re-mains of the game booth he was standing in and the one across the way, which featured half-size basketballs and hoops. The music of a carou-sel drifted down cheerily down from some dis-tance away, with carved elephants and horses and swan boats circling endlessly to a tune he almost knew.

There were so many things he almost knew, could almost touch. It was frustrating, infur-iating, knowing he knew things and unable to remember what they were.

He looked down at himself, and saw dirty overalls and a blue shirt with the sleeves rolled up. His left arm was sinewy and dark brown. The musculature of his right arm was noticeably less developed.

11

"Musculature"? Where did that come from?

He flexed the arm gingerly, rotating the wrist. Full range of movement, no apparent pain. He stretched the arm out, noted resistance. The arm had been favored for so long that the tendons were contracted, the muscles underdeveloped. Not beyond hope; full extension was uncomfortable but not impossible. A few weeks of steady exercise should restore it. It would take longer to build up the muscles, but it could be done with a simple weight program.

He looked down at his denim-covered legs, noted the difference in the thickness of his thighs. Once again, the right leg was noticeably thinner. There was a word for what he was seeing, but all he could remember was something about an iron lung.

There was more to it than that.

He couldn't remember how he knew that.

Instead of worrying at it, he'd focus on what he did know.

His name, for example, was not Bob. His name was Sam. It was the first thing he reminded himself of, every time—well, as soon as he had the opportunity, he corrected himself, prying a blue plush chicken from under a sheet of plywood. Sometimes things were a little too harried to think about anything when he first Leaped in somewhere. Like this time. React first, think second, then dust himself off.

He was here to do something. Wherever "here" was this time. Whenever "here" was.

He was a time traveler in a screwed-up experiment—"a little caca," as someone had once said; who, he couldn't at the moment recall. He wasn't originally supposed to actually travel, only observe. The Project was designed to find a way to observe the past, to let people be unseen observers of history as it was made. They called themselves "holograms," after the insubstantial images that were real holograms.

The process was nearly perfected by the late 1990s, when somehow, something had gone terribly wrong, and instead of being an Observer, Sam—Sam's mind, consciousness, whatever—Leaped, trading places with random people like Bob Watkins, putting his consciousness in Bob's body and Bob's in Sam's, thirty years—give or take a few—in the future. And to make things worse, either the process of traveling in time, or the flaw in the experiment, had punched holes in his once-photographic memory, leaving him only scraps of memory.

He brushed off a green rabbit, and sighed.

Judging from the way the kids dressed and the length of their hair, it was sometime in the fifties or early sixties, not earlier than 1953—according to the theory that said he couldn't Leap into a time before his own birth (and he was absurdly pleased that he could recall the year of his birth)—and not later than about 1962. He wrestled a piece of plywood up, still sneaking looks over his shoulder at the thin crowd for clues.

It was a game, of sorts, when he had the leisure to play it; find out as much as possible before Al Calavicci, his contact with his own time, traced him. What part of the past was this? And of course, why was he here?

Somewhere he could hear snatches of "Blue Suede Shoes," over a very poor set of loud-speakers. It was the fifties, all right.

"What's your name?" It was Bessa again, mumbling around the finger in her mouth.

Placing his hands on the counter, he leaned over. Bessa, sitting on a stepstool, blinked sublime blue eyes at him. He opened the flap and came around the counter, limping slightly, to crouch down stiffly beside her. From his new position, looking up at her, she was even prettier. She wore a grimy pink dress with a little white apron, and her face needed a handkerchief and a mother's spit.

"What's your name?" she repeated.

Smiling, he gently removed the finger from her mouth and wiped it dry with a corner of his shirt. "I'm Bob."

"No you're not."

Small children were always so definite about such things, he'd noticed. This one was no exception.

"Well, Aline says I'm Bob."

Her gaze became mutinous. She wasn't buying it.

Exhaling heavily, he surrendered. "Well, okay. I'm not really Bob. But Aline, and that other man—"

"Mr. McFarlan'," she supplied instantly.

"Mr. McFarland," he repeated. "Yes. *He* thinks, and Aline thinks, I'm Bob. So we're going to pretend, okay? You know how upset grown-ups get when you try to tell them things."

Bessa nodded, her finger firmly back in her mouth, giving this careful consideration. But she was not a child to lose sight of the main point. "What's your name?"

He exhaled again, looking at the hand that balanced him against the counter side. It was shorter, squarer than the hand he remembered as his own, but it was—it was his hand, too. He could see his own hand.

His mind was still used to perceiving himself, even if he was temporarily resident in someone else's body. He blinked, and the world stabilized.

"Are you sad?" Now she was worried. "Did you get an owie when the ducks fell down?"

A twinge in his hip told him he was probably fibbing, but he said, "No, I'm not sad, and I didn't get an owie. Are you lost, Bessa? Is your mommy around here?"

She shook her head again, long straight hair whipping across her cheeks in her determination. "You're not Bob. What's your name?"

It was never gentlemanly to argue with a woman, even if she was only four years old. He had to answer sometime; she wasn't going to give up. "My name is Sam. Sam Beckett. But don't tell anybody, okay?"

15

She cocked her head and studied him, and he put on his best trustworthy expression. "Why?"

Oh, Lord, please don't let her start asking Why. "It's a game. Like with the ducks. But just you and me. Okay?"

"Okay." With that, she scrambled down from the stepstool and ran away, vanishing into the jumble of hot dog stands and try-your-luck games, and he levered himself wearily to his feet and surveyed the wreckage. "Oh, boy."

More people were wandering down the midway, peering at the remains of the booth and at the man standing in front of it. He could hear them commenting. Oh, it was a mess, all right. If only they knew how much of a mess. With an uncharacteristic flare of temper he kicked at a board, almost lost his balance. Someone laughed.

It was an uncomfortable reminder. Bob had some physical problems, with the arm and leg. There were some things he probably avoided doing. Kicking things would be one of them. Sam would have to be careful about that. Once he figured out what he was supposed to do, Bob would be back. He'd hate to leave the poor guy with too much explaining.

But he was so *tired* of having to figure out what he was supposed to do. He wanted to go home.

He wanted to remember home, for starters.

He pivoted, deliberately turning his back on

16

the ruins, and surveyed the rest of the world he'd been thrown into.

Against the horizon, a pink neon arch spelled out "dlroW ylimaF s'rebeahcS." To his right the glow of a Ferris wheel described bright circles against the darkening sky; to his left, against the red and yellow layers of sunset, the skeleton of a Loch Ness monster drew stark, undulating black lines. In between were games, vendors, clowns, music, wonderful smells, and not enough people. For a moment he considered pursuing the monster.

"What's the problem here? Good Great Harry, what the hell happened?" The speaker was a man in his forties with a weary expression on his face and a patch on his overalls that said "Schaeber's Family World."

Bob, of course, wouldn't go chasing odd things on the horizon; he already knew all about them. So he, Sam, had to stick around and do whatever Bob would do until he figured out what Bob did *wrong*, and then go fix it.

There was a finite chance that what Bob did wrong was follow orders and repair the game booth, and that he, Sam, was *really* supposed to go find out what that skeleton was really all about. But he doubted it. He took one more longing glance at it. It was already invisible against the rising night. Sam sighed.

"Uh, I fell." He waved his hand around at the mess.

"Hearing those voices again, son?" The man stepped past the counter and lifted a large piece of plywood out of the way. The question was obviously rhetorical. "Well, come along. Get ahold of that end there, okay?"

So Bob heard voices, did he? That might simplify matters. When and if Al ever showed up. "Yeah, well, I guess that's right. I was just— hearing things." He chuckled in a hollow fashion. "Seeing 'em too, I guess." Like a man pointing a gun at him.

The man stopped long enough to shake a graying head at him. "Now I've told you and told you, you shouldn't say things like that. *I've* known you all your life, and I know about you seeing things and hearing things. But you shouldn't talk about them. People won't understand."

You were the one who brought it up, Sam protested silently, but he took the other end of the board as directed and hauled it around and upright. Shrieking, the mechanism that rotated the ducks tore loose and fell off.

"Aw, hell," the other man said. "Gonna take some time to get this working again. I swear, Bob, more things been goin' wrong around you, doesn't hardly seem fair." He picked up one of the ducks, touched the pockmarks in the yellow paint where the BBs had hit the target, ran a finger along the cartoonlike beak and raised wings, pausing at the jagged edge. "This was one of Karl and mine's very first games, you know that?"

He sounded infinitely sad. The message was clear that Karl was no longer around.

"I'm sorry." As always, Sam felt the words were wrong, totally inadequate, and as always couldn't think of any that were better. Instead he reached out for another of the spoiled ducks and began stacking them as carefully as he could. The other man kept on studying the broken place on the one he was holding.

"Bob? Are you in there?" It was the voice of the woman, Aline, that was her name. "Oh, hi." The greeting was directed toward the other man. She was not in a position to see the sudden whitening of the man's fingers as he clenched the target. Sam could.

"Yes, I'm here." Sam put the stack down. "I'm, I'm getting some help fixing things up."

Now that the adrenalin wasn't flooding his system, he could see that Aline was a very attractive woman. The dust had been brushed out of her dark hair. One eye was still bloodshot, but the other was a lovely violet. She had a creamy clear complexion models would kill for.

A vagrant question wandered through his mind—where did he know a model from? He could almost remember— No. It was gone.

Probably one of Al's girlfriends.

Like most of Al's girlfriends, she was paying very little attention to him.

"I can see that," she said. A wisp of hair drifted across her forehead, and she batted it out of the way, exasperated. "Jesse, did you bring by those

19

receipts? I can't find them in the office."

The man on his knees must be Jesse, then. He didn't get up or even look around. His voice was remarkably even. "I've got the receipts, Aline. In my office. With the account books."

Aline inhaled and exhaled with the air of one counting to ten. "I asked you to bring them by, Jesse. How am I supposed to tell how we're doing if you've got everything?"

"You could ask me." Bristling, Jesse set the broken target down, got up and faced her. Sam tried to fade into the newly upright back wall. "Karl always asked me."

"Well, Karl's *gone*, and I need to see for myself!" Aline pulled in another deep breath and tried again, obviously attempting to placate Jesse's pride. "Look, Jesse, I'm sorry, but I really would like to go over those books. I know there's a lot I don't know, but you're the only one who can teach me. Please?" Her lashes batted in approved Southern Belle fashion.

It didn't work. "You don't need to know. Karl trusted me." Jesse looked her up and down. "But I guess everybody does things their own way. You want the receipts, the books, I'll bring them. Anything else you want?" His lips worked against each other.

Aline closed her eyes and shook her head, exasperated. "Thanks. That'll be fine for now."

Jesse marched past her, out of the booth, and down the midway. As he left, one of the remaining light bulbs snapped out. "Go get new bulbs,"

20

he ordered Sam as he left. "We can get that taken care of, at least."

"Where—" he started, but Jesse was already gone.

"There's a supply truck over by the office," Aline said absently, still looking after Jesse. "Dump the prizes you can save in there, will you please? You can put them up again tomorrow."

"Uh, yeah, sure." For some reason he couldn't articulate very well. It wasn't just the fact that she was a pretty woman that was making him tongue-tied; it was almost like a physical impediment. He wanted to ask her something leading, so he could find out more about where and who he was, but by the time he found the words she was walking away in pursuit of Jesse.

Aline left him with the diminishing lights, an armful of stuffed toys, a set of conflicting orders, and the problem of finding the office. And the truck.

If he were an office, where would he be?

By the entrance, no doubt.

And where would that be?

He really hated the first part of a Leap, fumbling around trying not to make a fool of himself. Time to make use of that much-vaunted intelligence he was supposed to have. The flow, or trickle, of people was from east to west, roughly toward the mysterious skeleton. Of course, there was an easier way to tell where the entrance was, one that required no intelligence at all.

Loading up what he already thought of as his good arm with the stuffed animals, he started toward the neon writing on the sky.

One of the booths he passed was labeled "Old Tyme Photographs." As he walked by he brailled through Bob's pockets with his free hand. No wallet, but a few dollar bills, some coins, keys. Not much in the way of clues. It would be nice if he could find a driver's license, complete with current date, picture, age. Maybe another card that said "In Case of Leap Please Notify—"

Where *was* Al, anyway? Did it usually take this long for Ziggy to locate him? He couldn't remember. Leaping did things to his memory. He wasn't even sure he could always remember the things he had already remembered once.

Or he thought he'd remembered once.

"If you weren't a stable personality to begin with, Sam Beckett," he mumbled, "you'd be nuts by this time."

Looking up at the Old Tyme sign, he made up his mind and marched up to the vendor. "I want a picture, please."

CHAPTER
TWO

The grainy sepia print showed a lean, wiry young man with an open, innocent, defenseless face, neatly trimmed short dark hair, and eyes that could have been any color at all. One arm curled protectively to his side, and something in Sam's blurred memory clicked and whirred and tossed up the words "neurological damage," with a question mark following.

He thought he remembered Al telling him once that he was a medical doctor, but he couldn't remember having a specialty, or his internship, and he certainly couldn't have been in private practice.

Something made Bob protect that right arm. Sam could move it, but now that he was moving around, he found himself reluctant to do so. It was the same side of the body as his aching hip, and he wondered how much of the pain was his and how much was Bob's body remembering pain. But it was his hip for the time being, and *he* wasn't lame—or at least he wouldn't be if he hadn't bashed himself trying to protect Aline against a nonexistent threat. At least he thought so. There was something inherently confusing about that.

Of course, his whole life had been inherently confusing for some time now, so he shrugged and tucked the picture away in a pocket and went looking for the office and the truck.

The office, dark at this hour, was a single-wide trailer parked not far from the neon-arched entry and admission booth. There was a double door at the top of three wooden steps, a metal screen and a wooden door behind it, and both were firmly shut. Behind it was a trailer truck with a padlock hanging by the open hasp. He edged the back panel of the truck open, dropping only one chicken in the process. Opening the door admitted enough light to find an electric lantern. The inside was filled with crates and boxes of supplies—including light bulbs, he was glad to find. He dumped the toys and picked several boxes of bulbs that looked like the ones in the duck booth.

The light bulbs kept his hands occupied while he tried to add up what he already knew. Bob Watkins was a young man. He worked at Schaeber's Family World, an amusement park, apparently running a target-shooting game and doing general gofer work. The boss was a very pretty young woman named Aline. And there was Jesse, who had mentioned someone named Karl—a former boss? Maybe he was meant to reconcile Aline and Jesse. Sam hoped not; they looked awfully far apart and likely to stay that way.

Then there was that jerk McFarland. He had to fit in somewhere. The memory of that laughter stung.

He loaded himself down with light bulbs and clambered out of the panel truck. Who knew, at this stage? Maybe he was here to teach Bessa not to suck her thumb. He needed Al, and Ziggy. And Al was taking his own sweet time about showing up.

As he left, he was interested to see that behind the truck a line of mobile homes were tethered to gas and water hookups. Housing for employees? Maybe this was where Bob lived. Since Bob's nonexistent driver's license also didn't have Bob's address, he could visualize himself doing a lot of hunting for someplace to sleep if Al didn't show up soon with some information.

By the time he got back to the booth, Jesse had returned and had most of the damage under control, the splintered panels neatly stacked. Sam placed the boxes of bulbs in an unsteady pile and held the canvas top in place as Jesse used a hammer and nails to fasten it. The older man moved around the little booth with the ease of long practice and comfortable skill.

"Put those under the counter," Jesse direct-ed, indicating the bulbs and a few animals Sam had missed the first time. "Out of sight, out of mind. I want to go over the damn 'coaster with you."

"The 'coaster?" Definitely one of the worst things about Leaping was the feeling of stupidity that haunted him until he figured out what was going on. Well, maybe it wasn't the worst thing, but it was damned close.

Fortunately, Jesse didn't seem bothered by his blank look, but just waved him to follow. Maybe Bob was slow?

No, Bob's intelligence was at least normal and probably above, judging by Jesse's running com-mentary as they passed the vendors and games.

"That pony hacker needs to get a farrier in this week, he's letting things go there. Did you take a look at the motor on that cotton can-dy machine? Miguel says it's still running too fast. I don't want that McFarland to hear him." Jesse's monologue began to take on the tone of a well-rehearsed complaint. "Damned smart aleck'll just tell Aline it's one more thing gone to hell. Miguel wants a new machine, but we've got no money for things like that. Ought to over-haul it. Karl ought to have known better than to leave all this to that little brainless wonder, putting all her money into this stupid—

"Ah, I shouldn't be complaining to you." With that they left the brightly lighted area of the

26

midway, and suddenly Sam realized that arching above him were the bones of the monster, an intricate wooden structure perhaps a dozen feet wide and rising from waist level to an altitude incredibly high, arching far above the trees.

He gasped with delight. It was a roller coaster, a wooden roller coaster, and he could trace the long steady climb to the first heart-stopping drop as it rose and blended into the darkness. The sign by the passenger loading dock blared, "RIDE THE KILLER DILLER—TALLEST ROLLER COASTER IN THE MIDDLE COUNTIES!"

Another mental click and whirr as he walked along the ground craning his neck at the rising track, squinting hard to see the top of the crest. His eyes widened as his gaze followed the drop, and his lips moved silently.

"Now, Bob, don't go talking to yourself again, I want to show you this. In case Aline decides she wants you working on this, too." Jesse chewed his lip. "Since she's making the decisions these days."

"This thing will be going at least fifty-eight miles an hour when it hits the bottom of the first drop," Sam said. He reached out to caress the heavy upright, staring up at the support beams lacing the sky over his head. The wood was warm and rough and fitted into the lines and curves of his hand. The track, lighted now only by a pair of spotlights, stretched steeply past the two men. A line of

27

lights showed how the ride would gleam and glitter when it became operational. It wasn't ready yet, but very little was left to be done. He could even smell the fresh paint on the cars.

Jesse stared at him. "Where do you get this stuff?"

"It has to," Sam insisted, certain without knowing why "Look at the angle of descent, and the height, there's an equation that—"

"What equation?" Jesse demanded. "What in the holy hell are you jabberin' on about now, boy?"

Sam opened his mouth again and the image of numbers, pure and elegant in his memory as if his hand had just written them on a blackboard, fled. "I don't—remember."

"Yeah, right." Jesse looked disgusted. "Well, that might be or it might not. All I know is, this thing is another damned waste of money."

"The lights should be on," Sam said. Another memory teased him—a county fair, sitting with his little sister in the very first car—it was a beautiful fall evening, he could look down at the upturned faces as they went up and up and up and the people below got smaller and smaller, the car moving through a river of lights fastened to the rails on either side. He'd just won the blue ribbon at the 4-H calf show and he was climbing to the stars with Katie giggling and screaming beside him. And then she was standing up and raising her hands as the car crested the top, and his heart almost stopped as he felt her slip out of his grasp. He snatched at her blouse and yanked her back into her seat, and she turned to him and laughed—

And the memory was gone. He couldn't remember what happened next. Couldn't remember the sensation of falling, of whipping around the turns and curves. He probably spanked his sister when they got back down, but he couldn't recall.

But the roller coaster gave him a good feeling, the feeling of climbing to the stars, so probably nobody got hurt. He'd remember, surely, if somebody got hurt?

"There you go again, daydreamin'. Can't keep your mind on things for more'n five minutes. Never could.

"Well, hell. It's getting too dark anyway. We'll look at this tomorrow." Jesse strode away, giving up.

"Yeah, daydreamin'." It was Al at last, mimicking Jesse's tone and expression perfectly in his own familiar, slightly raspy timbre. Jesse, of course, didn't hear. No one could hear Al except Sam. No one could see him either. The image of the small dapper man, interrupted by an overturned bucket where his right foot was supposed to be, was invisible. "You were always good at daydreaming."

Yesterday upon the stair
I saw a man who wasn't there

Al Calavicci was a real person. Over the past few years Sam had come to accept both his reality and his invisibility. At the same time Al was the only person who accepted Sam's reality, too, the only person who called him by his proper name no matter what or who he looked like. The physical Al stood in a room in a laboratory in the middle of nowhere some thirty years in the future, give or take a few. Somehow he was linked to Sam. "Brain waves" had been mentioned. There were few details. Details, Al had given Sam to understand, would be against the rules.

Sam belonged in that laboratory too, in charge of the Project code-named Quantum Leap.

The theory was great. The practice was another matter.

Since the experiment went wrong, Al was the only continuity left to him. Al was his reality check, his validity monitor. At some level now he needed Al, once just his best friend, more than breath or vision or gravity. Without Al to remind him who he really was, he would be left unable to trust his own sanity.

He wasn't there again today
I wish to heck he'd come to stay. . . .

"Hey, Sam!" Al was shaking the handlink, the mechanical link to the master computer. A cylinder of ash split off the massive cigar in his other hand. Instead of hitting the ground, it

30

separated from the cigar and vanished.

Momentarily lightheaded with relief that Al had finally appeared, Sam ignored him, his gaze still following the tracks of the Killer Diller. He could hear the chirping of the handlink as Al poked at it. Al never could cope with small machinery—he was really better at the administrative end of things, but that was not something you told an engineer. Anybody could do administrative work, engineers claimed.

Sam vaguely remembered knowing better, but Al's failures to communicate with a piece of inanimate machinery were comforting somehow, like a—like a what? "A flatplate transceiver that always flickers when you turn it on. You know it's going to work, but there's always that flicker to let you know nothing's perfect." Somebody had said that once.

So what was a "flatplate transceiver"?

"I hate roller coasters," Al announced, evidently winning the battle with the machine. "Remind me of flight training. They'd put you in and drop so many G's on you you'd black out. Sam? Are you listening?"

"Yeah, I'm listening. Isn't it great?" Sam continued to walk, stumbling against a loose plank and barely catching himself against one of the track supports. "Did you ever ride on a roller coaster, Al?"

Al snorted. "I used to work on one of these things. When I was sixteen. I hated them."

31

"Oh, come on. They're terrific. You get up so high—"

"And you fall so far."

This time his tone of voice got Sam's attention. He swung around to give Al his full attention.

Something *was* wrong with the handlink; now Al was hovering about six inches above the ground, and part of his left leg was an iron strut. Even though Sam knew he was seeing an image, it was still unnerving. There was something to be said for some kind of shimmer in holograms, just so you'd know where you were with them. Or, more accurately, where they were with you. Al's image didn't shimmer at all. He looked—present.

He was wearing a relatively subdued—for Al—electric-blue suit with wide iridescent-purple lapels that caught the multihued light from the handlink and gave him the effect of glowing in the dark. It was just as well nobody else could see him, Sam decided.

Of course if they could see him, they'd probably think he was just a clown who'd wandered off the midway.

Al's expression was still grim. He glanced over their heads at the framework and grimaced. "That thing must be over a hundred feet high."

"Not quite, but close. Okay, where and when am I? What does Ziggy say I have to do?" This was it, the information he had to have; he didn't like the way Al was stalling. It usually meant things were bad. Very bad. Even worse than usual.

Sam couldn't remember why he had walked into the Accelerator, months or years ago. He couldn't remember the details of the theory that allowed him to believe that he was being shifted around from life to life within his own life span. He did know, through sometimes painful practical experience, that each time he woke up in someone else's life, something had to change. So far, he had always managed to make the change. But Ziggy the computer postulated, and he had no reason not to believe, that if he failed to change whatever it was that had to be changed, he would be trapped forever in another person's life.

He would never get home.

Al hemmed and hawed and focused on the handlink, squinting at the tiny readout. "Well, let's see. It's July 10, 1957, a Wednesday, and you're in Jasmine, Oklahoma. God, I didn't know they made towns this small—well, I guess it isn't *that* small—"

"Could we cut to the chase, Al?"

He had to believe that if he made enough changes, he would get home again—whether it was because he needed to change the world into something he could live in, or because the process of Leaping was teaching him things he needed to know for some further, mysterious purpose still hidden from him, he did not know. The Project he had believed was defined and

33

bounded by science had become something else. Something or some*one* was directing his destiny as if he were a puppet, moving him from place to place without ever asking his opinion. Yet even that Power had, or chose to have, limits if Ziggy was right, because Sam could still fail.

The punishment for failure was permanent exile.

Al had guided him away from the roller coaster, closer to the lights and bustle of the amusement park, and was still frowning over the handlink. With people around, even though they couldn't see him, the Observer cheered visibly. "I *like* carnivals," he observed. "I remember one time, there was this really gorgeous blonde, and we took a ride through the Tunnel of Love. . . ."

"*Al.*" If Sam allowed his one link to his own life to get sidetracked by memories of lost lusts and temporary loves, they could be here all night. They could be here for several nights. Al had a wealth of experience to be sidetracked by. "*Al!*"

"Oh. Yeah. Well. You're Bobby Watkins, twenty-three years old, and you work at—"

"Schaeber's Family World."

"Yeah, right."

"So what am I supposed to *do*, Al?" The people Al was so glad to be around were beginning to look at Sam sideways as he pried information out of the invisible Observer. He changed a grimace into a smile and a frustrated gesture into a wave. A ticket seller hesitantly returned the greeting.

Al heaved a long-suffering sigh. "Okay, okay. It's that roller coaster. The Kill—" He batted at the glowing machine, trying to keep the data line from hanging up.

"The Killer Diller." Sam was impatient with the limits of the screen on the little control. He made a mental note to tell Al to tell Ziggy to redesign it, make the screen bigger. There was some reason it was so small, but he couldn't recall what it was.

"Yeah. Killer Diller. Well, it sure is that. Because the Killer Diller is going to kill seven people on its grand-opening ride on Sunday. Four days from today. And Ziggy says you're here to stop it."

CHAPTER

THREE

Aline Schaeber shuffled the stack of receipts on the table, compared the total to the month's electricity bill, and rubbed her eyes. One still burned from the mishap at the duck booth, and both were just plain tired from staring for hours at columns of figures, debits and credits, outgo and income.

It wasn't enough. It hadn't been enough for quite some time, even before Uncle Karl started getting sick. That was the one comfort in the situation; she hadn't inherited Family World and run it into the ground. It was well on its way before she ever got it.

She shuffled the papers again, trying to make the sums add up differently. It didn't work.

Getting up from the kitchen table, she went over to the stove and poured herself a cup of coffee and leaned against the sink, considering. If she could just put off paying for a few more days, the opening should cover the worst of the outstanding bills. The trouble was, she was paying people as well as the electric company and the bank, and people had outstanding bills too. It wasn't just her problem, it was the problem of every person who depended on a paycheck from Schaeber's.

The carnies would move on at the end of the season, taking most of the games and the pony rides and the life with them. But the vendors and the people who operated the rides—they lived in Jasmine year round, they had to feed families. Most of them had worked for Karl for years. Even the carnies, the itinerant vendors, they'd come season after season. The old man had considered them family. Part of his Family World.

Now they worked for her, and they were her responsibility. And if she was going to keep them working, she had to find some way to bring people back into Family World. Developers could come waving fistsful of money to buy the land Family World stood on, tear it all down and build a factory. Some kind of space stuff, like the Russians were supposed to be doing. But no one in Jasmine, none of the people who worked at Family World, was going to find a job in a factory like that.

A noise at the front door caught her attention. Listening, she could hear Vera grumbling down the hall from the dining room to the door. Voices at the door became louder as someone came in.

Vera appeared in the doorway with Mike McFarland behind her, blocking his way. "Mr. McFarland came to see you, Aline," she announced unnecessarily. Her lips were thin with disapproval. "I told him it was late."

"I know it is," the sandy-haired man said with an easy smile. When Vera didn't move, he stepped around her. "It will just take a few minutes."

He paused significantly, but Vera stood her ground, drying her hands on her apron. She must have been putting up flowers in that old crystal vase in the dining room again, Aline thought. The vase had been cracked for years, but Vera insisted on using it.

"I think Mr. McFarland wants to talk business, Aunt Vera," Aline said gently. "Please don't worry about us. I know you had things you wanted to do."

It was as tactful a dismissal as she could muster, but Vera was outraged nonetheless. She spun around without another word and marched down the hall, heels crashing against the wide-planked wooden floor.

"Mike, please sit down," she went on. She would rather deal with McFarland in the front room, but since he had followed Vera to the kitchen instead of waiting in the foyer, courtesy demanded she make him welcome. "What on earth would make you come out so late?" She hesitated, anxious suddenly, and got up to get another coffee cup for her visitor to hide it. "There's nothing wrong with the ride, is there?"

"Just black, one sugar," McFarland said, watching her steadily, and it made her uncomfortable. "No, there's nothing at all wrong with the ride. I checked it over. That's why I'm here."

She turned to see him moving the bills back and forth with the tip of a finger, smiling to himself, and felt a flash of resentment. Setting the cup down in front of him, she swept the pile of paper to one side, ostensibly to make a clear place on the table between them. The fact that it also moved the bills out of his reach didn't escape his notice, and he grinned openly.

"This is quite an operation for such a pretty lady," he said, sipping. "Mmmm, you surely do make a good cup of coffee."

"I think of it as a family business," she replied, ignoring the obvious flattery. "What's on your mind, Mr. McFarland?"

He set the cup down again and rotated it back and forth, switching the handle from side to side. "Well, as I said, I've gone over the ride. And it's in absolutely tip-top condition. Perfect working order. It's going to give a lot of people a lot of pleasure, that Killer Diller. I'm really proud of it. It's almost, you might say, the achievement of a lifetime."

40

She warmed a little at his obvious pride. "I'm very pleased with it."

"It's going to do you a lot of good."

She hesitated, searching for some oblique meaning, but could find none. His light brown eyes were open and frank now, and held no hint of ulterior motive. Despite herself, she responded in kind.

"We have to find a way to bring people in, Mike. We've tried lowering the prices. Offering door prizes. Renting for parties. They all worked for a little while, but not well enough or long enough. The Killer Diller had *better* do us a lot of good. The opening should have been on the Fourth, but with Uncle Karl dying—" Her voice caught, and she stopped.

They looked simultaneously at the pile of bills.

"Are they dunning you?" he asked, and almost immediately raised a hand to forestall her reply. "No, I'm sorry, that's none of my business. Absolutely none. I wish—" Pausing, he tilted his head as if to consider his words carefully, then moved it back and forth as if to negate his thoughts. "No. No, never mind." He pulled out a fold of paper. "I just came by to tell you that I consider my work finished, and I can leave anytime. Your ride will be open at last on Sunday." He slid the paper across the table to her.

"What?" For a moment Aline was shocked speechless, taking the offering without looking at it. Of all the things she had expected, this was the last. "You're leaving?"

He arched his eyebrows. "Well—"

"I don't know what to say," she said. Then she opened the fold of paper.

It was a bill for seven thousand dollars.

"That covers my time, and the roller coaster design, and the materials," McFarland informed her. Now his eyes were like flint, his tone defensive. "If you'll review the contract I had with Karl before we began the project, it's due and payable upon completion. Karl signed it. It's legal. You can't set it aside."

"But, but—" she sputtered, and got up in confusion to get another cup of coffee without having finished the first. There was no money. There was no way she could come up with a check for seven thousand dollars. It was more money than all the other bills combined. It was a fortune. It was impossible. At Karl's funeral, and afterward, McFarland had never mentioned money. She had always assumed the ride was already paid for.

Maybe I really am as bad at this as Jesse thinks I am, she thought. *How can I pay him? He wants his money before he goes. He's entitled to be paid. The laborer is worthy of his wage.*

By the time she had emptied the cup down the drain and refilled it she had her composure back. "I won't hear of your leaving," she said, returning to the table. "Absolutely not. This is your achievement, and you should be here to see

42

it open. I really want you to stay."

"Do you, Aline?" His voice lowered, became softer, and she could feel her face become warm.

"Well, of course I do, Mr. McFarland. Besides, you've been most helpful in other odds and ends around the park. I really don't see how we could do without you the next few days." She took a deep breath. "And I would feel so much better if you took the time to review the ride once more with Jesse and Bob and some of the others. I just don't know how we'll get along once you're gone."

They were words that could be taken as gushing politeness or as an invitation, and for a long moment it seemed her visitor was considering which way he would choose it. Then Aline leaned forward, her cup forgotten between her hands.

"This ride is going to make all the difference, Mr. McFarland. It is terribly important to me. And it's a triumph for you, too. I think you should be here to see it open. And, from a strictly business point of view"—she paused to make sure he knew she meant it—"it makes good sense for you to stay. I won't hear of your going until after the ride opens." *And I can pay you this simply extraordinary amount of money*, she thought wildly.

He laughed, throwing back his head so that the sandy hair caught the light. "All right. I have to confess, I was hoping you'd say that. But I did want you to know it all checks out.

43

As of this moment, you own one of the most thrilling—and safest—rides in the Southwest." He glanced at the pile of bills. "Or the bank does. It's quite an undertaking for a beautiful lady. Must be quite a strain."

"Only until the opening," she insisted stoutly. She rose and held out her hand to him, and he took it and kissed the back of it gallantly.

"To the opening," he said. "You have no idea how much I'm looking forward to it."

Vera, standing in the doorway, had seen the last exchange, and glared until McFarland dropped Aline's hand and submitted to her draconian escort out. Behind him, Aline's smile became uncertain and faded. That last remark about the bank was unnecessary, surely. He didn't have to remind her how precarious things were. She already knew. She had tried everything she could think of, everything she had learned from Karl, from other park owners who didn't know from her letters that she was a woman, and a young one at that.

Now she was grasping at one last straw. Something different, something the Middle Counties hadn't seen. Something new. Thrilling. Dazzling.

The Killer Diller.

She looked at the bill in her hand. Seven thousand dollars.

And if the ride didn't bring in the people, Schaeber's Family World would fold. And that would be that. She would have failed all those people depending on her. She would have failed Karl, the big bluff hearty man who had been a father to her. She would have failed her own dream of a magical place where an orphaned, lonely small girl could walk, tiny hand securely tucked into a grown-up's, and have lights and music and joy. She could remember the first time she had ever visited the park, when she had been that little girl, and her amazement that such a wonderful place could be real, could belong to her Uncle Karl.

Now it was not only real, it was hers, and while the magic was a little tattered around the edges, it was still alive. Somehow she would keep it that way. It would not only be alive, it would flourish. More than anything else she wanted it to flourish. It was her heart's desire. She blinked, her bloodshot eye stinging suddenly.

She sipped at her coffee. It was cold.

Someone had once said that you could tell everything you ever needed to know about a person by looking at their bookshelves. Sam had always felt that there was a sweeping, untested assumption in that premise: the person under examination had to *have* bookshelves, for a start. As far as he could tell, Bob Watkins didn't have any. He hadn't read a book since high school. And maybe not even then, according to Al.

"He's the local crazy," Al said, popping in again without any more warning than usual.

"Sees things, hears things, talks to people who aren't there."

"I can identify with that," Sam muttered. He always felt as if he were snooping in someone else's life, going through their homes, their possessions, violating something integral to their lives and to his own as well. It was like—well, it *was*—walking into someone else's home uninvited.

Sam had tried to follow Jesse at the Killer Diller, only to find that the older man was gone. That had left him with the problem of locating Bob's home. Going back out into the main part of the park, he had wandered around more or less aimlessly, listening to Al explain how much, or how little, information they had on the accident. So far, the computer's review of history only showed an accident would happen. Further information would be forthcoming, Al assured him, scowling at the handlink.

Meanwhile Sam exchanged greetings with vendors and game operators. Evidently Bob was well known and well liked. Eventually he found himself wandering around the trailers behind the office, wondering how he was going to figure out if Bob lived in one, and if so, which. Ziggy the computer was no help. History showed that Bob Watkins' legal address was a post office box, which would be a little cramped for sleeping.

He was hoping for a discreet sign that said "Watkins," when inspiration struck; he went back to the duck shoot booth and grabbed an unwieldy stack of light bulb boxes from under the counter, and asked the nearest carny to help him get them home. The ride operator looked at the empty carousel, shrugged, and stepped forward to help him out. Sam lagged behind, capitalizing on Bob's limp, and the friendly native guide led him directly to Bob's front door.

"Real lucky for me," Sam continued, laying on the sarcasm. "If Bob goes around 'seeing things,' at least people should just take me for granted when I talk to you. No problem. Piece of cake."

"Uh, not this time." Al was really uncomfortable about all this. His gaze kept sliding away from Sam's, and he poked at the handlink much more vigorously than usual.

Sam turned away from his inspection of the closet and gave Al his full attention, raising an inquiring eyebrow.

Al cleared his throat. "Well, you see, Bob's kind of got the reputation of being, sort of, you know, well, things keep going wrong around him. Like the booth."

Sam winced at the reminder and rubbed his hip. It still hurt. He hadn't had to exaggerate Bob's limp much at all. "So?"

"So, when the 'coaster crashes, well, they think—" Al waved one cigar-laden hand around. Sam could never understand how a man as concerned about the outside environment as Al could do so much damage to his internal environment with those damned cigars.

47

He remembered once challenging him on the subject, and Al responding with a lofty quote about consistency being the something of tiny minds. At least since Al was only an image, Sam didn't have to put up with the smell. "They think you did it," Al finished.

"And?"

"And what?" Al made a great fuss about poking at buttons on the handlink, not meeting his eyes.

"What else?"

"What do you mean, what else?"

"You're holding something back, Al, I can tell. What is it?"

Al surrendered ungracefully. "They think Bob caused the crash, but because he's crazy, they don't send him to jail. They—"

"Put him in an asylum," Sam whispered. A cold chill crawled down his spine.

"Where he dies, ten years from now."

"Oh, God, no." He could remember, in flashes of physical memory, a former Leap: crawling between the bars on a bed. The binding of a straitjacket, helplessness, unable to move his arms, to even balance when he walked. People staring at him as if he were some species of wild animal. Others around him, babbling mindlessly, eyes wide and staring, incontinent, the meaningless noises out of mouths that should be able to talk and laugh and sing. The smells of urine and feces and sweat and loneliness, of ammonia and cement walls. The explosions of

48

pain that they called therapy.

Incoherence. The slipping away of identity, of knowledge of himself as Sam Beckett, of knowledge of himself as a man, as human.

The fear. The greatest fear he could know was the loss of his ability to think. He thought, therefore he was. He could accept gaps in his memory in the faith that someday they'd be filled; he could piece together his life around a core of self-awareness. But without the ability to think, he was, literally, nothing. The only thing left of Sam Beckett was mind, and if that was gone, he faced obliteration.

To be trapped for the rest of his life with the mentally ill, treated as one of them—and what could he say that wouldn't be considered madness?—in the facilities available in this time and place, would inevitably drive him as mad as the rest.

"They think *Bob* did it?" he said, his throat suddenly dry. He licked his lips, trying to bring out some moisture. "That can't be right. People here know him. You saw it. They're all his friends. He's harmless. A little clumsy maybe—"

"I think they were looking for a scapegoat." Al was trying to be reassuring; he even walked through the table and tried, uselessly, to pat Sam on the back. "*I* know you didn't do it."

"But that doesn't matter, does it? I can't stay here, Al. I have to get out."

Their eyes met, an entire conversation in one glance. Sometimes Sam was tempted to stay in whatever life he'd Leaped into, quit changing things and let history just happen, live the life of the person in whose body he found himself. Some of the lives were normal, relaxing, relatively wonderful ordinary lives.

A life in an asylum would meet none of those criteria.

"Ziggy says there's a ninety-seven percent chance you're supposed to stop the roller coaster from opening."

"Does Ziggy say how?" Sam looked down at what was in his left hand, a once-white cotton shirt he'd been holding when Al had popped in. His hand was clenched tight. He deliberately relaxed it, welcoming the distracting pain as blood rushed back into his fingers.

"We're trying to find out. The records aren't very good. But you've got—this is Wednesday night—three and a half days. That's something."

"That isn't enough." He closed his eyes, trying to erase the shards of memory, replace them with something else. It didn't work. He opened them again, looking around the bedroom, just big enough to hold a bed and a dresser. Above the battered dresser a mirror hung, and he looked into the eyes of Bob Watkins. Bob looked terrified too.

"I'll see what I can do." Jabbing at the handlink, Al summoned the Door to the future and stepped through.

Sam stretched out on the bed, staring at the empty space where the Door had been. The heat in the trailer was awful, even though he'd opened the tiny windows. A ceiling fan pushed eddies of hot stale air around and around.

He remembered:

Katie, standing and raising her hands to the sky, screaming in delight and then protest as he hauled her back into her seat. Her laughter. His deathlike grip on the safety bar in front of them. The faces far below, round white dots looking up at them, whipping past too quickly to see as they plunged down, up, around, back and forth as if the cars were animate and determined to shake their occupants loose.

It was such fun, riding a roller coaster.

He could visualize—he didn't think it was a memory, not a real one—a body shaken free, arcing down. Aline Schaeber's body. Landing limp and broken in the middle of the white upturned faces.

Himself, begging for something he hated and feared, because if he didn't he would never see Al again. The anguish on Al's face as the Observer goaded, beseeched him to ask the people around him to hurt him. That was a real memory, an incomplete one because he couldn't remember what he was begging for or what came next. But he could remember how it felt.

And it was a memory he didn't want. Sometimes his swiss-cheese memory could be a blessing.

His stomach coiled, and he lurched off the bed and into the tiny bathroom and vomited into the toilet.

Some ten minutes later he had rid himself, or Bob, of everything Bob had eaten in the past three days, and hung gasping on the edge of the sink.

"All right," he said, startling himself with the rawness and decision in his voice. "All right. That's enough."

Bob's image looked back at him, eyes red-rimmed, face pale. He wiped his chin with the back of his right hand, noted clinically the reflected deterioration of the muscles in the arm. He flexed the hand experimentally, watching the way it responded in the mirror. Yes, the arm was a little stiff, but usable. Pretty much the way he felt himself.

He'd take the metaphor. "I am Sam Beckett," he said, as if reciting a pledge, or a prayer. "I am a scientist. I founded Project Quantum Leap. I'm here to do something, and I'm going to do it. I am not going to end up in an asylum. I'm going to go home.

"I *will* go home."

Someday? a corner of his mind pleaded. *Someday will You let me go home*?

Thursday

CHAPTER FOUR

On the world stage in the year 1957, Israel and Jordan accepted U.N. peace proposals. Forty-six people died in an attempt to overthrow the Batista regime in Cuba. The Common Market was born. Tail Gunner Joe McCarthy died. The neutrino was produced at Los Alamos Laboratory. Antineutrinos were discovered. The Defense Department told America her major cities would be guarded by Nike Hercules missiles. John F. Kennedy won the Pulitzer Prize for his book *Profiles in Courage*. Albert Camus won the Nobel Prize for literature. A bitch named Laika orbited the Earth. The Dodgers abandoned Brooklyn. The 102nd element, nobelium, was discovered. Dr. Seuss wrote *The Cat in the Hat*. *On the Beach*, and *On the Road*, appeared in bookstores, and *Visit to a Small Planet* appeared on stage. A playwright named Samuel Beckett presented a play called *Endgame*.

In Jasmine, Oklahoma, on Wednesday, July 10, 1957, the temperature had hit 102 degrees for the second day in a row, and Sam Beckett, who did not remember any of this except nobelium, woke in a stranger's bed and prepared himself once again to face a stranger's life and a stranger's future.

Al Calavicci, who did not remember any of these events either but had had all of them brought to his attention in a quick review of history during the night, stood next to Sam as he brushed his teeth. The bathroom was small enough that he appeared in the torn shower curtain instead of in front of it, with a faded fish fluttering in and out of his hunter's-green lapels.

"The trouble is that Jasmine, Oklahoma, just isn't very important," he was explaining. "Ziggy's having trouble nailing things down."

"But you know the accident's going to happen," Sam mumbled around a mouthful of toothpaste. He had felt queasy once about using other people's toothbrushes. Several Leaps back he had decided any germs involved would be as confused as he was and probably die of indecision before he could pick up an infection. So far, the theory seemed to work.

Rinsing, he spat out the foam and wiped his mouth, reached through Al for a towel. "Do you mind? It's a little crowded in here."

"Huh? Oh, sorry. I guess I'm just used to talking to you in bathrooms." In bathrooms, people couldn't see Sam talking to apparently empty air. Al stepped outside. "Anyway, yeah, the accident happened. It was the biggest thing in this part of the state for years. The park closed down. Developers bought up the land but never did anything with it. Jasmine finally just died away."

"Does Ziggy have any ideas about how the accident happened? Or how to stop it?" The sight of Al standing in the middle of the bed— not *on* the middle of the bed, but *in* it—stopped him cold for a moment. Gamely, he went on, "Or anything at all?"

"Er, no."

"Great. Just great." Sam started opening drawers in the dresser, looking for socks.

The top drawer held a photograph album. With Al peering over his shoulder, he began to page through it.

"Hey, who's the fox?" Al chirped.

"The what?"

"Fox. Isn't that the word they used now? Or then?" Al was beginning to get fuddled in the tenses. "Or was it chick, or babe . . ."

Sam ignored him, studying the photos—page after page of pictures of Aline Schaeber. The very first one in the book was an elementary school group photo, with a caption scrawled in faded pencil reading "Aline and me together." The other thirty-some children in the class might not even have existed.

There were more class pictures, then newspaper clippings of Aline at a cotillion, at the seasonal Park openings, at Fourth of July picnics. There were no more of the laboriously handwritten captions.

"Wow. She's pretty." Al could always be trusted to cut to the heart of the matter.

But Sam didn't need a second opinion. He closed the book, thoughtfully. "Yes, she is."

"Hey, do you suppose our friend Bob is fixated on her? Maybe he really did do something." Al was beginning to get apprehensive as the pages turned.

"No." Sam didn't know where the certainty came from, but it was familiar and he always trusted it. "No. He's crazy about her, but it's not that kind of crazy. I think Bob has a crush on her. Maybe even loves her."

Al shook his head, made a tsking sound. "Love can get warped." When Sam refused to accept it, he warned, "You could be wrong, Sam."

The last few pages of the album were blank. He started to put it away, but misjudged the distance to the dresser. It slipped, and another, folded yellow clipping fell from the back of the book. The newsprint had been creased shut so long that the process of teasing it open caused it to crack along the fold.

It was an obituary for Mrs. James Watkins, widow of James Watkins who had died bravely at Omaha Beach. She had died of cancer at the age of thirty-nine, survived by her only son, Robert James, age sixteen. Flowers were requested at the Jasmine Home of Final Rest.

"Oh, man," Al said sympathetically.

Sam closed his eyes briefly, folded the scrap, and placed it carefully back in the album. "Al, it can't be. If Bob was the one who caused the accident, then when I Leaped in, the accident couldn't happen anymore, could it? Because Bob wouldn't be here to do it. And *I'm* certainly not going to. So just being here, I would have prevented it from happening, and Leaped out. It's not that simple. It's never that simple."

Replacing the book and all its dreams and memories, he slid the drawer shut and continued looking for socks that matched. "Besides, if that was all it was, I wouldn't have had to Leap in four days ahead of time. I'd only have to be here for the period of time that the mistake happened in."

"Assuming it was a mistake, and not deliberate," Al argued, grasping for the last intelligible thing Sam said.

"Assuming Bob did it. So he didn't. It couldn't have been Bob." Finding a pair, he pulled them on, laced on the heavy work boots that had been shoved under the bed.

Al frowned, mentally turning the argument one way and another, failing to find a flaw. "I hate it when you get logical."

"Look, I *know* he didn't. In my gut."

59

"I hate it worse when you get emotional."

So am I wrong? Sam's expression said. "I think we have to assume it was an accident, and the best way to prevent it is to prevent the opening. That means I need to convince Aline not to hold the opening."

"But it's already been announced. She's not going to believe you just because you say it's going to crash."

"I'll just have to convince her. It would help if you could find out exactly what went wrong," he added.

"I hate it when you get sarcastic, too," Al muttered, glaring at him as he opened the Door and stepped through.

"Me? Sarcastic? Never," Sam murmured to himself, smiling.

"What, never?" Al's voice floated back, as the Door slid down.

"Well, *hardly* ever." Sam began to hum to himself.

He couldn't just walk up to someone and ask where Aline Schaeber lived; Bob would know already. On the other hand, if Bob was a little crazy, maybe that might be the best approach. It didn't appeal to Sam. He headed for the office, looking for a telephone book.

The blades of a large fan flapped lazily behind the desk, providing a welcome stirring of air. The temperature was already climbing through the eighties. The paper scattered over the desk was limp from the humidity. A girl of about six-teen, dressed in a wide skirt and pink blouse, her mouse-brown hair strained back in a ponytail, was chewing gum and examining her nails.

"Kin I he'p yu?" she said, without looking up.

"Need to borrow a telephone book," Sam mumbled.

"Who you want to call?" she said incuriously, still not looking up. A hangnail on her left index finger held her complete attention.

"That's not—look, can I see the phone book, please?" Sam clamped down on the irritation he felt.

" 'S raht theah." She rotated one shoulder at the bookshelf behind her.

The drawl was a little too thick to be true.

"Thank you." Sam moved around the desk.

"Don't know what you need it for," she con-tinued. "Y'could just dial any ol' number at all. They're all the same." With a tiny grunt, she pulled the hangnail away, examined the result-ing dot of blood, and stuck the finger in her mouth. She looked a little like Bessa, except that Bessa's eyes were more intelligent.

The girl yawned, without covering her mouth.

On second thought she didn't look in the least like Bessa.

Unfortunately, the 1957 telephone book in Jasmine provided only the exchange, FLower, and the five-digit extensions of the subscribers. Addresses were not provided. Four Schaebers

61

were listed; none of them were named Aline or had the initial A. Stymied, he put the book back.

"Told you they was all the same," the girl mumbled around the mouthful of digit.

Opening the door, Jesse stuck his head in the office. "Bob? There you are, I've been looking for you. Dusty needs some help with those damn ponies of his. And don't forget about the farrier. Get on over there, will you?" Jesse looked harried as he entered. "M'linda, did anybody come in here?"

"Not while I've been here." The girl giggled. " 'Cepting Bob, o'course, but he don't count."

"Thanks," Sam told her. Melinda, completely absorbed in her now-wrinkled finger, ignored him. Jesse waved him on, and he went out again, looking back as he did so. Jesse was standing at a filing cabinet, going through some papers. Melinda was yawning again and waving a languid hand in the air. Sam waved back before realizing the gesture wasn't aimed at him.

He remembered seeing the ponies not far from the Ferris wheel, and headed that way. An elderly caramel-apple seller smiled at him as he went by and he returned the greeting, feeling better about things.

"Got a little hitch in your gitalong?" Al appeared out of the ether and fell into step beside him.

"Huh? Oh." Sam became aware that he was still limping, reached back to rub his hip. His arm didn't respond as easily as he wanted it to. "Must have hit it harder than I thought last night."

"Either that or Bob's brush with polio when he was a kid."

"Polio?" Sam looked down at his right arm, remembered how it appeared in the mirror. Not crippled, but—withered.

"There was a big epidemic before the Salk vaccine. Little epidemics almost every year. I remember reading a book called *The Man in the Iron Lung* about a guy in his twenties who caught it on a trip to Hong Kong or someplace. He was completely paralyzed from the neck down." Al shook his head. So did Sam. Al never ceased to amaze him. He would never have suspected the other man would be interested in reading what sounded like a quintessential story of hope and life affirmation. Then Al went on, puzzled, "The guy got married and had a couple of kids. Never could figure that part out."

That explained it.

"So Bob had polio?" he asked, as much to divert his friend from the distraction he was obviously intent on pursuing as to find out more about Bob. Any second now Al was going to ask him when penile implants were invented, and he was damned if he wanted to talk about it.

"Yeah, but it wasn't bad. He lost a year of school, and his right arm and leg are a little weak, but that's it."

"Did you find out anything more about the accident?" With a start, Sam realized that one of the vendors running a basketball game was eyeing him oddly. He gave the man a sickly grin and a wave, and was relieved to see him shrug and sort spare change into the red and yellow apron all the game operators wore.

"That guy doesn't care," Al said. "They all think you're—I mean *Bob*, is a little nuts anyway."

Sam shot him a furious glance. "Just what I want, right?" It was hard to talk without moving his lips. He wiped away a line of sweat on his forehead, deliberately using his right hand to do so. It wasn't hard, he told himself. It was *his* hand, after all. Not Bob's. "You still didn't say if you found out anything."

"Ziggy's looking," Al protested, aggrieved. "It takes time to find out things about places like this. We're working on it. We've got a little.

"Robert James Watkins was born in 1934. Same year as Aline," Al added parenthetically. "His mother died in 1949. He was taken in by Karl Schaeber and Karl's sister Vera for two years. Nice folks. They'd taken in Aline when she was only four and raised her, too. Karl gave Bob a job at Family World and he's been working here ever since, doing odd jobs. He's got that reputation of being a little 'off.' Seeing things, hearing things.

"That's all I've got so far, Sam. It's going to take a while. Sorry."

64

"I don't have much time." To a ticket seller who gave him a quizzical glance he added, "To get my job finished."

"We're doing the best we can." The handlink squealed as if in agreement. Sam stopped to stare.

"It never did that before."

"What?" Al, with his best approximation of innocence, batted at the multicolored machine. "Make noise? Sure it has. Does it all the time."

"Is there something wrong with the handlink?" Sam said between clenched teeth. A worse possibility occurred to him. "Is there something wrong with Ziggy?"

"No, of course not. I'm here, aren't I? We've got a real strong contact, no question about it." The handlink squealed again. Sam tried to grab it, forgetting momentarily its lack of substance, and ended up shoving his hand through Al's throat. "Hey, watch it!"

Sam took a deep breath, counting to ten. "Why is it making that noise?"

"How should I know? *I'm* not a scientist."

"It's an engineering question."

"And I'm aeronautical, not mechanical." Al could look insufferably smug when he wanted to. "So I don't know."

"I give up." Sam stalked away, turned the corner, and almost tripped over a shaggy chestnut Shetland pony that was busy rubbing its hide against the rail fence to which it was tethered. In another pen five more ponies snorted and milled in the morning heat. Huge black horse-flies buzzed around them, and the ponies' tails slashed busily.

"Hey, boy, watch out there!" The cowboy on the other side of the ring got up from his moth-eaten easy chair, alarmed. As he did so, Al, still hammering at the handlink, caught up with Sam. The chestnut pony snorted and balked. Al, not noticing, kept on going, walking through the rail fence. The handlink let loose with a particularly ear-shattering screech.

The pony gave a screech of its own, reared, and crashed into the fence, breaking three boards and sending a post into a crazy lean. Dusty yelled. Sam yelled. Al looked up, bewildered, as Dusty barreled through him in an effort to cut the pony off at the newly created pass. "Damn it, get back here you little misbegotten bundle of dog food!"

"Who, me?" said Al.

Sam lunged for the pony, who whirled and kicked, accurately but without quite enough reach. Sam felt metal-shod hooves the size of his palm brush against his sternum and past his cheek just as he belly-flopped into the pony ring. The chestnut pony, a wicked gleam in his eye, bolted through Al and the hole in the fence and cavorted down the Midway, sunfishing with every other stride.

"Bob, why is it that things just keep falling apart every time you show up?" Dusty said, slapping a tattered Stetson against leather chaps.

Dusty was an old, weathered man with skin that looked like it could have been carved from oak and night-black hair. His chaps looked like they had seen use on a working ranch, and his hat was stained and battered.

"Good question," Sam said through gritted teeth, glaring at Al. Al shrugged, glanced worriedly at the handlink, punched at it. The Door opened behind him and he stepped through without another word.

Which was, as far as Sam was concerned, still two words too many.

"Good question," someone else said, laughing. "Man, you are some kind of jinx!"

"You got some business here, McFarland?" Dusty was looking hostile.

McFarland chuckled and stuck his hands in his pockets. "Hey, Dusty, haven't you noticed how every time the gimp shows up things break down? Machines must like him. They want to be just like him. Lame." Laughing at the joke, he sauntered away. Dusty spat into the dirt.

Sam struggled to his hands and knees, spitting unpleasant things out of his mouth, trying to apologize, when the air blurred in front of him. He blinked, and blinked again, trying to focus on something that seemed to dance just out of the edge of his peripheral vision. For a moment he could have sworn he saw—

"What is it?" Dusty was standing over him, offering him a hand. "What?"

Sam swayed as he got up, even with the supporting arm. "I don't know." Alarmed, he looked down the Midway. The little horse had long since disappeared. "The pony's gone—shouldn't you get the pony?"

"Hell, yes, I'll get the pony. What I want to know is, what's wrong, boy? You don't look right. What did you see?"

"I didn't see—" Sam stopped, started again. "The pony's eating caramel apples."

"At Leezie's stand?"

Sam nodded, not knowing what he was agreeing to but knowing that he was supposed to nod.

"Well, there you go. If *that's* all, let's go get 'im." Dusty slapped his thigh again, reached for a halter hanging on a still-upright post. "Unless you want to tack up the rest of 'em."

Sam looked around at the rest of the ponies, huddled into the other pen, their eyes rolling and ears pinned. "Leezie's, you say?"

"That's what *you* say," Dusty informed him, striding down the Midway. Sam scrambled to keep up with the older man's long strides.

"But how do you know—" he began.

"Look, boy," Dusty growled at him. "Maybe those others don't pay attention, but my momma was a fullblood Choctaw, and she taught me to pay attention when folks like you go seeing things."

Sam decided that this would be a good time to shut up and think. He had a sinking sensation he knew what Dusty meant by Bob "seeing things," and he didn't like it at all.

He liked it less when they rounded Leezie's caramel-apple stand and found the pony busy munching down the stock, tail switching in bliss as the elderly lady flapped her skirts in futile fury at him.

"Go get around his other side and be ready to grab that lead," Dusty directed him.

Obedient, Sam circled, waving a hand to calm down Leezie, who refused to be calm. He was just in time to see Dusty move into position, see the white-ringed eye roll in his direction, and duck as the pony charged, a freshly dipped apple still in its mouth.

They chased the pony, who was hugely entertained by the process, through most of the amusement park before it consented to be cornered against the operator's booth of the Killer Diller. Sam could have sworn the animal was laughing at him.

"Did you see that critter bolt on you?" Dusty demanded, as they led the now-docile pony back to its fellows.

"Yeah, sure," Sam answered. "I was right there—"

"Then why'n hell didn't you say so? I coulda gone around instead and we'd have saved chasing this damn piece of dog meat all over creation."

Wincing, Sam realized that when Dusty asked him if he had "seen" the pony bolt, he didn't mean when it had actually happened. He wanted to know if Sam—Bob—had known ahead of time.

Which meant that Dusty believed Bob *could* know.

Which meant Dusty believed Bob was psychic.

CHAPTER
FIVE

Sam spent the rest of the morning repairing the pen, grooming ponies, and saddling and leading them around and around in circles inside the repaired pen. Dusty sat in his overstuffed chair and took tickets, glaring occasionally at Sam. He still hadn't forgiven his helper for not being one jump ahead of things. Sam decided not to mention the farrier—the ponies' hooves looked good enough to him. He'd had a close enough look to satisfy himself.

Finally Dusty got up, peered at the blazing sun overhead, and nodded. "Time to take a break."

"Thank God," Sam muttered under his breath, sagging against the fence.

"What you think you're doing, boy? Go get the hose and fill up that trough. These beasts been working all morning. They need water. Not too much. Get to it, boy!"

A good cowboy always takes care of his horse first.

Even if the horse only came up to his belt buckle. Leading the little herd one by one up to the trough, he let them drink, tried without success to keep them from slobbering all over his pants. The chestnut pony appeared to take particular glee in nuzzling up. Remembering the ring around his eye, Sam was careful to keep away from the little monster's head.

"I'll take you personally to the slaughterhouse if you even try," he warned.

The pony snorted.

"Hi, Sam."

For a moment Sam didn't react to his own name. It took another repetition before he looked up, startled. It was Bessa, finger firmly in her mouth, standing on the bottom rail and peering at him between the top and second ones as she used her other hand to hold on. She was wearing a threadbare blue pinafore dress and white socks with matching blue trim, and single-strap white patent shoes covered with mud and manure.

"Hi there, Bessa." Making sure the last animal was securely tied, he threw a glance at Dusty, who looked at the little girl and turned away, elaborately signaling that he couldn't care less if Bob wasted his break talking to the child.

"How are you today?" Sam went on, hunkering down to bring himself to her eye level. It was getting to be a habit with Bessa—somehow you had to deal straight with her. Since hunkering didn't quite work because of her perch on the rail, she obligingly stepped down.

"I'm a good girl," she announced.

"I'll just bet you are." Sam tugged at the pacifying hand and wiped the finger clean. Bessa promptly put it back in her mouth. "I'll bet you're a big girl, too. Big girls don't suck their fingers."

"Yes they do," Al said from behind him, jabbing his cigar for emphasis. "I can remember . . ."

Sam shot him a don't-you-start look. "Don't listen to him," he told the little girl.

Bessa looked from man to hologram, blue eyes wide. "Big girls don't?"

"No," Sam said firmly. "They don't."

"Then I'm not a big girl," Bessa decided, and shoved the finger more securely between her lips.

"Gotcha there," Al chortled. "You may not be a big girl, but you're sure a smart one," he told her.

She smiled a smile full of sunlight at them both.

"Hey there! We got customers waiting!" Dusty's shout brought the two men about. Three little boys even younger than Bessa stood with their parents at the opening to the round pen, clinging to adult hands and watching the ponies—horse-sized to them—with wide eyes.

73

" 'Scuse me," Sam said to his audience, and went over to help Dusty perch the boys up on the saddles.

"I like him," Bessa confided to Al, who remained beside her to watch.

"Yeah, I like him too." Al took a drag on the cigar, realized it was cold, and patted his vest pocket for something to light it with. He was wearing a red suit with a white, black, and red silk shirt, discreetly ruffled. He became aware that Bessa was looking at him critically.

"Are you a clown?" she asked.

"No, I am not a clown," he responded with dignity. Failing to find matches or a lighter, he stuck the cigar in the inner pocket.

The handlink shrieked. The nearest ponies threw up their heads, eyes rolling. Sam hauled down one pony that he'd been about to put a child on, and Dusty grimaced and moved away. Bessa clapped her hands over her ears, removing them only when she was sure that awful noise had gone away. "You *look* like a clown," she informed him in a severe tone. Sam snorted and got a new pony, smiling at the child's parents in placating fashion. The child, who saw himself as a buckaroo, objected to the more placid mount and was overruled. Al made a surreptitious adjustment, and the next squawk was more subdued.

"That's not a very nice thing to say." Al was used to comments about his wardrobe, and rarely minded it. However, he always paid attention to constructive criticism from the fairer sex. He couldn't help glancing back down at the little girl. Bessa was still watching Dusty and Sam. "Do you really think I look like a clown?"

Bessa nodded without looking up.

"Hmph." Al gave her another long look, then punched the Door code into the handlink. Lights blinked and the handlink hummed without result. Al tried bashing it against a post and succeeded only in waving it through six inches of wood. Finally he slapped his hand against the machine in his hand, and the Door opened.

Bessa spun around to stare at the rectangular hole in reality. "What's *that*?"

"That's my special door," Al told her. "I've got to go home for a little while."

"Can I come?" She bounced toward the Door, passed through it. After a moment she looked around the side, mightily puzzled. "It isn't there." She came around and marched through the Door again, her lower lip stuck out stubbornly. The same thing happened.

"You can't go through," she told Al. "It's just a shadow."

"Well, yes, to you it's a shadow. To me it's a door."

"Can *you* go through the door?" Her expression made it clear that she wouldn't believe him if he said he could.

"Yes," said Al, who knew that expression from long experience. "I really can."

"Take me." *Prove it*, she was saying.

Al shot a look at Sam, who was now going

75

in circles with a gray Shetland and trying very hard to keep a straight face. "Oh, shut up, Beckett. I'd like to see you explain it to her." He paused. "Though come to think of it, you probably could." Sam continued leading the pony at a sedate walk, chortling quietly. The child balanced on the saddle looked from him to Al, not understanding.

He turned his attention back to Bessa, who had her hands on her hips, waiting.

"No, honey, you have to stay here." He crossed glances with Sam, who nodded farewell. "I'll be back real soon. I promise.

"I hope," he muttered as he stepped through. "Gushie!" he hollered. "You've got to get this thing fixed!"

Jasmine, Oklahoma, was gone. Al was in a room sixteen feet across that appeared to glow coldly with blue-white light. There were no windows. Panels six feet long by three feet wide at eye level in the walls contained a gelatinous substance that shifted and flowed with speckles of glittering colors, the largest of the biocircuits that were Ziggy. On one point on the perimeter a door in a hexagonal frame slid upward, revealing a ramp which led to another, circular room. An eighteen-inch-thick wall shielded the Imaging Chamber from the rest of the complex.

Al stepped through the door and it slid shut behind him like a slow guillotine. Around the perimeter of the next room men in white coats moved back and forth, exchanging worried comments. None of them spared a glance at Al.

The center of the room was occupied by a large table made of translucent, many-colored squares. It was a much bigger version of the handlink, and it hummed. The squares glowed, red, yellow, blue, illuminating the shadowy circuits and connections within them. The lights brightened and dimmed in no apparent pattern. As if in harmony, the giant blue-silver globe suspended above it shimmered erratically.

Deep in the core of the table's pedestal, three squares were dark and silent, and their contents were invisible to the casual observer.

From beneath the table, a muffled voice said, "I'm trying, sir. I'm still not sure how to get to the damaged circuits without disassembling the whole control, and if I do that—"

"You may not be able to get it back together again." Al leaned over, trying unsuccessfully to see what was going on. "Every time you test something the handlink screams like a tortured cat."

"I can't help that," the owner of the voice said with as much dignity as he could muster. From the awkward position he currently occupied, it wasn't much. "I'm a programmer, not a hardware specialist. This isn't in the microcode. I think it's the special circuits, sir."

Al snarled, "I know, I know—We need Tina. Any luck finding her?"

Beneath the table, Gushie cleared his throat. "Er, no, sir, we haven't."

"Isn't there *anybody* else we can bring in?"

"Nobody who's cleared, sir." Gushie heaved a gusty sigh. "Nobody who understands the circuits." There was a pause and an ominous clatter, followed by a muttered oath. "Nobody understands these circuits," he added mournfully.

"Terrific." Al straightened up and strode out of the room, chewing his lip. From under the table came a relieved groan, a clatter, and another oath.

Opening out onto the Control Room was the Waiting Room. This was where the people Sam "replaced" came, conserving energy across time. Al didn't begin to pretend to understand the theory; Sam did, and perhaps two other people in the world did, but not even Sam was sure about that, since the other two weren't cleared to discuss it anyway.

Al hated it.

It wasn't the theory that made Al uneasy. It was what—or who—waited there. He summoned a lifetime's willpower, closed his eyes, filled his lungs, and stepped in.

The Waiting Room was a high-ceilinged hospital room the size of a small intensive-care ward, with an observation deck high in one wall, reachable by a short flight of stairs. The windows of the observation deck jutted out at an angle, giving the occupant or occupants an unobstructed view of the rest of the area.

The "ward" contained only one bed.

In the bed, a body lay, staring blindly up at the

78

ceiling. Al could only think of it as a body, even though he could see it breathing; he didn't recognize the person *in* the body. He didn't recognize the attitude of the body. He knew why the right arm was curled up tight against the chest, because the mind in the body still thought the body suffered the effects of polio. He knew the right leg was crooked under the sheet for the same reason.

And he could understand why the intelligence behind the eyes was in terrified retreat.

It was part of his daily ritual. Every day that he was at the Project, for years now, he walked into the Waiting Room to see the body of Sam Beckett and the mind of some other person half-mad with terror, and he said the same thing: "We're trying our best to get you out of here, kiddo. We're trying our best to get you home."

He was never quite sure whether he was addressing the body or the mind.

The physical shell of Sam Beckett appeared to be in his late thirties or perhaps his early forties, with pale skin that hadn't seen the sun in far too long. Bob Watkins currently occupied that shell. He didn't respond to Al's presence. He was hooked up to a series of monitors which were duplicated in the observation deck.

On the other side of the room, an elegant black woman wearing a white lab coat sat at a desk, tapping a pen against a pad of paper. When Dr. Verbeena Beeks had signed on to Project Quantum Leap, she had expected to do research in the psychology of a genius. She hadn't planned to be a practicing psychologist, holding the familiar hands of multiple strangers. With her usual grace and style, she had adapted without a murmur of complaint. Al, for one, was profoundly grateful, even if he didn't like to show it.

"Well?" he said.

"I don't know," Dr. Beeks replied. "He doesn't seem to be responding at all. I'm not sure if we should even expect him to respond anymore. All the tests I've run support your hypothesis, however."

"Do they," Al said thoughtfully.

Another voice, petulant, strained, and scratchy, seemed to come out of the walls around them. "The hypothesis has an eighty-three percent chance of being correct."

"So he really is psychic."

"The probability is within acceptable limits," the voice without a body said.

The doctor smiled tiredly. "Ziggy's really not taking this well," she said. "It resents the possibility that psychic ability even exists. Something it got from its parents, no doubt."

Al sneered, without enthusiasm. "I suppose I ought to take that personally? *I* never said psychic ability doesn't exist. So if Ziggy's taking after me, he shouldn't resent it at all." He gnawed on his lower lip. "Can we use it somehow?"

Verbeena shook her head regretfully. "Not if

I can't get through to him. And I'm not sure what we'd use it for."

"If he could—" Al hesitated, mentally trying out and discarding scenarios. "Ah, hell. I dunno how we can use it either. But there's got to be a way. I mean, he's got to be psychic for a reason."

Verbeena smiled. "Does he?"

Al's response was lost in another bioelectrical scream. "Gushie! Ziggy! Cut it out!"

"I can't help it if someone's poking around in my circuits like a ham-handed NeanderTHAL!" With the last word Ziggy's voice rose into an unintelligible wail.

"Gushie, whatever you just did, stop it!" Al yelled through the observation deck door.

After a moment, silence prevailed.

"And how is Dr. Beckett?" the doctor asked, breaking the moment.

"The last time I saw him he was leading a little kid on a pony ride. Kind of like we're doing here. Going around and around in circles. Have *you* heard from Tina?"

"No." She gave him a stern look. "You're the only one likely to know where she'd have gone."

"How was I supposed to know she was going to run away in a snit? How was I supposed to know Ziggy would break down in the middle of a Leap? How was I supposed to know . . ."

"That's enough of feeling sorry for yourself, Admiral," the doctor said firmly. "I'd like you to

81

review the list you made of places likely for her to go, and see if you can add to it. Meanwhile, I'll continue to try to establish communication with our friend Bob, here, and Gushie will do what he can to fix Ziggy."

"Do we know anything more about the accident?"

She shook her head, her long earrings swaying. "Have you explained our problem to Dr. Beckett?"

"Of course I haven't explained our problem to Dr. Beckett! What am I going to say, *Oh, by the way, Sam, I got into a fight with Tina, and Ziggy threw a circuit, and we're not sure we're getting any information on this Leap*?"

"That would probably be contraindicated for his feeling of security," the doctor agreed.

"It doesn't do a whole lot for mine, either." Al pulled out the cigar and bit into it, hard. "It would be nice to know if he was going to make it through this one. Maybe, if Bob really is psychic, he could tell us the future. His future. Whatever."

"It's our past," Beeks pointed out. "Ziggy should be able to figure it out eventually."

"But it keeps *changing* on us." For a moment, despair filled Al. To hide it from the astute perception of the psychologist, he strode over to the bunk and stared down into the open, unseeing eyes. "Are you sure he's even in there?" he asked over his shoulder.

"Those are not Sam Beckett's brain waves,"

the doctor replied with calm conviction. "Perhaps it isn't Bob Watkins, but it most certainly is not Dr. Beckett."

"Don't even suggest that," Al snapped, shuddering. "Things are bad enough as it is." As if to underscore his remark, another unearthly wail came from Ziggy.

The doctor winced. "It sounds like it's in such pain."

"I *am*," Ziggy answered. "And I'm not an 'it.' "

"Of course you aren't, Ziggy," Al soothed by reflex. He took the cigar out of his mouth, studied the body on the bunk again. "Come back, damn it," he said, soft enough so the doctor couldn't hear. "We need you back."

The body did not respond.

"Sam—"

"Did you say something, Admiral?"

"No. No, nothing." He looked around again at the Waiting Room, let go a long breath as if he had been holding it the entire time, and turned to go. The doctor held out a clipboard for him to sign, and he scribbled a signature on it as he walked out.

"Where are you going, sir?" Gushie said from under the table. "Are you coming back?"

"Yeah, I'll be back. I'm just going to change clothes." He wasn't sure, but he thought he could hear the programmer mutter, "Thank God."

"Everybody's a critic," he snarled. "No appreciation, that's what it is. Nobody appreciates me."

• • •

Mechanical things under stress, twisting, splitting, shattering, snapping. Shards of metal, bright jagged edges. Gears grinding, jamming, straining against each other, toothed wheels gnawing helplessly against each other. Pieces meant to be linked which fell away from each other, flailing independent and wild. Processes stopped. Movement ended.

And the people, the silly soft people that depended on the machines without understanding how they worked, trusted them to function without attention, without care, were caught in the inertia of motion, the laws of energy and action and reaction that were the only real laws, and they paid for their ignorance with terror and screaming and blood. So much blood.

Blood, he thought, was the lubricant of ignorance. The more ignorant they were, the more blood would be required.

He liked keeping things oiled.

He liked reminding the ignorant that there was a price to pay for power. There was a price to pay for not paying attention, for not giving credit where credit was due. If they wouldn't recognize him for what he was really worth, he would remind them.

And it felt good to remind them.

He had been snubbed once too often in his life, and he would have to remind them once and for all.

CHAPTER SIX

Sam peered up at the sun, trying to figure out the time from its position. Bob, it appeared, didn't own a watch. It was the middle of the afternoon, and miserably hot. Not even standing in the shade made a difference. Too humid, he thought, and wondered if being somewhere dry would help. He could remember dry heat from somewhere, but that particular memory didn't help—it couldn't change the way things were now. Dusty, rolling a cigarette, cocked a weary eye at him.

"You feelin' poorly, boy?" The question was meant in kindness, but it probably also meant Sam had overlooked something.

"No, I'm feeling fine." The ponies were snuffling noisily in their feed bags, the sweat marks from the saddles were almost all gone, the tack was all neatly hung up. The ring had been scraped clean, and large green flies buzzed lazily over the muck heap. The smell of horse sweat and manure hung in the air like a mist. It was a little like being on the farm again. He blinked at a sudden vivid memory of brushing down his father's only horse, a chestnut like the escape-artist pony. Sam's father had been a firm believer in up-to-date machinery—the horse was a sentimental leftover.

The resemblance between pony and horse ended there; the horse had been one of the draft breeds, and he'd had to stretch tall to get the withers. There had been a collar scar on the big guy's neck, and he always brushed it gingerly, even though he knew the sore was long healed, because the horse remembered.

He'd been about ten years old.

He couldn't recall the horse's name.

"You look like a critter that's been spooked. You been using that arm of yours a lot. Hurtin'?"

It *was* hurting, he realized, rubbing at it. It felt like his arm—the fingers massaging it felt like his fingers. He had to remind himself they weren't. Bob Watkins' body was only on loan. He'd better be more careful of it.

And he'd better not let himself be distracted from what he started out to do.

"No, it's fine." He shook his head at the flat bottle that Dusty held out to him, then changed his mind. He couldn't afford to antagonize a

86

possible source of information. "Thanks."

The whiskey went down smoothly, then lit a fire in the back of his throat. He coughed, tears starting up, and handed the bottle back. "That's good stuff," he wheezed.

"Ain't horse piss." Dusty seemed pleased at his endorsement. "Siddown, boy, you make me weary lookin' at you."

Sam collapsed on a hay bale and slumped back against a convenient railing, recalling too late that he had neglected to find out where to get breakfast that morning. He spent a precious few minutes working up enough saliva to swallow the taste of the whiskey. His head was buzzing a little.

"Well," he started, cleared his throat, and began again. "Well. You've been around a long time, haven't you, Dusty?" He figured it was safe enough for Bob to be familiar; a number of the parents had called Dusty by name, and so had one lanky teenager.

"Long enough."

"Do you like it?"

"What'n hell kinda question is that?" Dusty took a long swallow from the bottle, offered it to Sam again. He shook his head, carefully.

"Thanks, I better not. That's powerful stuff."

Dusty snorted like one of his own ponies, accepting the excuse. Sam brushed at the streak of dried red clay on his shirt, the result of his fall. Flakes came away, but the shirt underneath was stained vermilion. Judging from the dearth of clothing in Bob's closet, he'd have to find a laundromat before he Leaped out, too.

"I mean," he said, "what with—" he almost said "Aline," decided at the last moment that Bob would be more formal—"Ms. Schaeber running things now, and all."

Dusty cackled and spat off to the right of Sam's boot. "*Mizz Schaeber*, is it? Haw! Now that's funny, boy. I don't reckon getting all formal with the lady is going to do you one bit of good."

"Well—" Sam shrugged, thinking furiously. Dusty appeared to assume that Bob was interested in Aline. Okay, that made sense in light of the photograph album. Unfortunately, it meant that Bob would naturally know where Aline lived. It would look odd if he had to ask.

Of course, he ought to be used to that by now.

"I heard she was going to move," he said, wishing Al was around. Al was a lot better at basic cunning than he was. Still, it was worth a shot. "She thinks that house on, on—" He paused as if fumbling, inviting Dusty to leap in, as it were, with the information he needed.

And for a change, it worked. "That old house on Mulberry Street? Where'd you hear that? That little girl's not going to move. She can't afford it, no better than you or me. Besides, where'd she move to? She's damn lucky she's got the house. Karl left her the whole works. Never mind who got cheated in the process," the cowboy added darkly.

"Who got cheated?" The question came naturally, before he had a chance to think about it, wonder if Bob would already have known.

Dusty, more than willing to talk as he kept an eye on the potential customers passing by, pulled a pouch of tobacco out of a back pocket and cut off a plug. Sam swallowed and directed his eyes elsewhere as Dusty tucked the brown fiber into his cheek, forming a lump the size of a golf ball. It was bad enough having to put up with Al's cigars, but he'd learned to live with it, secondhand smoke and all. At least they'd found a way to remove most of the carcinogens from the fumes. But chewing tobacco—Sam fought to restrain the urge to vomit as Dusty sent an initial dark brown stream into the red dirt.

"Well, there's some as think Karl meant Jesse to take over," the cowboy began. The lump in his jaw didn't interfere with his talking. Sam wondered how long the man had been chewing, and how long it would be before the tumors appeared. He closed his eyes and turned his face to the sun, stretching his arms out along the rail behind him. After a moment he decided it wasn't quite comfortable, and pulled his right arm in again. "Jesse, he practically started this place. It was his land to begin with. Didn't know that, did you?"

"No, I sure didn't," Sam replied with absolute truth.

"Yep," Dusty said comfortably, slumping down to absorb the unrelenting sunshine like a cat. He was one who loved a good story. "Jesse's kin homesteaded this place clear back in the Land Rush, lived here ever since. Had to sell off some, o'course, when the Depression hit, and then the dry times. That's where Karl got into it."

He cocked an inquiring eye at Sam. "You sure you don't know all about this? Y'ought to, boy."

"Well, somebody might have said something, but I really don't remember." Sam kept to the literal truth.

Dusty spat. Sam winced. Dusty went on, "The Schaebers, they were always canny folk. And that Karl, he was the smartest of them all. He bought up land all around the place. Then when the Bartletts got into the revival business, letting the preachers throw their jamborees in the fields where the Bartletts couldn't grow nothin' anyway, Karl Schaeber rented out tents to 'em. He sold Jesse on putting in kiddy rides. They was partners for a while.

"But Jesse, he never was no good at running a business, kept losing money, and Karl kept bailing him out until Jesse didn't have no interest left."

Dusty spat again. Sam tightened his eyes and tried to imagine a revival meeting, benches set up on the hard-packed earth, lanterns to push back the darkness, a huge tent packed with sweating people, paper fans rustling, people murmuring, and up front a man in a black coat and string tie waving his arms and yelling hoarsely, book

90

in one hand and index finger of the other jabbing at the sky. The man he visualized had a wiry build, somewhat below medium height, with dark hair, snapping black eyes, and a long cigar in the jabbing hand. He stifled a grin.

"You think that's funny, a man losing his land that way?" Dusty had seen the grin and misinterpreted it.

"Oh no, of course not. It's a shame. But Jesse still works here."

"Yep. Thinking all the time, I'll bet, that when old Karl finally kicks the bucket, he'll do right by him in his will. After all, Jesse was practically running the place all by himself. But what does Karl do but leave the whole shebang to his niece. A lot of people think it's not right."

"Including Jesse?" Sam asked artlessly.

But Dusty achieved belated discretion. "Can't say about that."

"I know that Aline wants the receipts and such turned over to her now. I heard her ask Jesse for the books." Sam was trying to coax the other man into more revelations.

Instead, Dusty creaked to his feet. "Aw hell, I forgot about that. I got some of those. You stay there, boy." He disappeared into a small shed behind the pens.

Now that the vision of chaw was gone, Sam could look around again, and he did so, rubbing at his arm. There was nobody at all in the Midway now except Family World employees, probably because of the heat. The ponies stood somnambulant, hind legs cocked up, snoozing peacefully, the only indication that they were even alive the swishing of their tails at the flies. Some of the games had pulled shades down, screening out the sun, making it obvious that they didn't expect business anyway.

He hoped things would pick up for Dusty and the others as the day stretched into a long summer evening. With this humidity, though, it probably wouldn't cool down even after sunset. He rolled his head back against the rail again, wondering if he was getting Bob sunburned. For the moment it was very peaceful. Even the tinny proto-rock and roll from the speakers seemed far away. The snuffling of the ponies in the hay was a lot closer.

After a while Dusty came back with a thin envelope, tattered and stained. "You take this to 'Mizz Schaeber,' " he leered. "Give you a chanct to see her again. Tell her there ain't much there because there ain't no kiddies to ride. If her rolly coaster don't change things, I don't know what all I'm gonna do."

The envelope didn't look as if it contained much. It didn't feel that way either as Sam took it. His concern vanished, however, as he realized that Dusty, or someone, had written out an address in painfully elegant copperplate writing: Miss Aline Schaeber, 4 Mulberry Street, Jasmine. He was almost dizzy with relief. Or maybe it was lack of food. He had to eat soon—

92

being sick last night and having eaten nothing today was definitely having an effect on him.

"You get me a marker now, you hear? Don't let her forget again."

"I won't," Sam assured him. Now all he had to do was find Mulberry Street. In a town the size of Jasmine, that couldn't be too hard.

"She forgot to give it to me the last time. Jesse never forgot."

"I'll make sure you get it," Sam said again, and started down the Midway.

"Hey, what you going that way for? You walked in too many circles today, boy? It's that away!"

CHAPTER

SEVEN

The streets in Jasmine were shaded by arching
tree limbs, and the leaves washed the sky with
a gentle murmuring. The houses were huge and
wooden, vaguely Victorian in prim white with
green or blue shutters—none of the riot of color
usually associated with turrets and bay windows
and gingerbread. Every house seemed to have
a porch with a swing. Sam walked along the
gutter—there were no sidewalks, at least not in
this part of Jasmine—quietly enjoying the shade
and the breeze and the glimpses of children in
rubber-tire swings and gray squirrels swarming
up trees. The air was thick with the lazy buzzing of bees. There were very few cars visible,
the air smelled of cut grass and roses instead of
gasoline, and it was quiet without being silent.
He liked it.

Jasmine was far from perfect, he knew. Even a small town in Oklahoma in the fifties would have had its own version of apartheid, with Darktown and Indians on the other side of the line of demarcation, separated from each other as well. There would be poor people of three races, each equally afraid and contemptuous of the others. But for this moment, walking down Mulberry Street, he could allow himself to forget social injustices and breathe deep of sweet-scented air. This Leap was to prevent an accident. That was all. This one was easy.

With address in hand, finding the house wasn't nearly as hard as he originally thought it was going to be. The Schaeber house was two stories plus an attic, with a wraparound porch like the others. Unlike most of the others, a stained-glass fanlight graced the top of the front door. He couldn't find the doorbell. Suddenly hesitant, he opened the screen door and knocked on the wooden inner door.

No one answered. He knocked again, wondering what he would do if no one answered. Go back to the park, probably, and try again later—

"Robert James Watkins, just what do you think you're doing?"

The woman who answered the door was not Aline Schaeber. She was easily in her sixties, looked older. Heavy powder and bright red lipstick failed to disguise the paper-thin, wrinkled appearance of her skin. Her fingers, still gripping the edge of the door, resembled claws. Her nails, coated with matching polish, added to the illusion. She was wearing a black dress with a white lace collar, and it made her look incredibly frail.

"Hello," Sam offered, feeling foolish. "Is Aline—Ms. Schaeber here?"

"And what does that have to do with the price of tea in China? Have you become a preacher, coming to the front door like this? You go around to the back this instant." With that the front door slammed, making the screen jump in its frame. The little woman was stronger than she looked.

Wincing, Sam walked around the porch, only to find that it didn't go all the way around. He had to come back to the front and go down the steps to get to the back of the house. The porch, and after the porch the side of the house, were lined with neat flower beds ablaze with flowers and humming with bees. The weight of the humid air was almost tangible.

A series of four wooden steps without a railing led up to another screen door. The wooden door behind it, which had four panes of glass, stood open. The woman was nowhere in sight. He waited a moment or two, then realized that he was dealing with a true stickler for the proprieties, and knocked in what he hoped was an acceptably humble manner.

"That's better," the woman sniffed. Sam could have sworn she was hiding behind the door, she popped up so quickly. She went on to greet him as if the encounter at the front door had never occurred. "Bob Watkins, how nice to have you come by to see me again. Won't you come on in and have a glass of lemonade?"

The back door led through a tiny mud room and into the kitchen. A white icebox that looked far too small groaned in the corner, and a ceiling fan managed to make the heat bearable. A braided rag rug took up most of the center of the room; a wooden table and chairs sat on it. Through a doorway he could see the dining room, far more formal with a dark cherrywood china cabinet partially visible. This was the house that had taken Bob Watkins in for two years when his mother died, he reminded himself. A part of him belonged here. This lady was probably Vera Schaeber, sister of the deceased Karl.

And Bob had spent two years sharing the house with Aline, who was by that time a year ahead of him in school, and whom he adored, at least if the collection of pictures and clippings was anything to go by. Now that was an interesting thought.

The woman produced a plate of oatmeal and sugar cookies and a pitcher of lemonade with a glass. "Now, you sit right down there and tell me what brings you all the way out here from that park," she said, bustling around to get herself a glass as well. "It has been a month of Sundays since you set foot in this house, I declare."

"I was hoping to see Ms. Schaeber," he said, taking a deep draught of the lemonade. It wasn't as good as his mother's—he smiled inside, delighted that he could remember the taste of his mother's lemonade—there wasn't enough sugar in it, and his mouth felt as if it were shriveling from the tartness. There was a yellow pottery duck on the table that looked like a sugar bowl. Maybe he could sneak a spoonful when she wasn't looking. He munched a cookie, suddenly aware he was starving. He wondered when Bob had last eaten.

"Now don't you go calling her 'Mizz Schaeber,' Bob Watkins. She isn't so high and mighty as all that, though there's some as thinks so. What did you want to talk to her about? You know you can tell your Aunt Vera."

Well, at least he was right about her identity. Not that she could easily have been anyone else. Aunt Vera—and thank Whoever for the quaint Southern habit of self-referencing, he thought, and then wondered where that stray bit of information came from—leaned forward like a predatory robin with its eye on the disappearing end of a worm. He had the feeling if he didn't speak up soon she'd spear him.

"Nothing real important," he temporized, licking a crumb off his lip. "I've got the receipts from the pony ride. Dusty asked me to bring them by. Is she here?" He wondered how successful he was going to be in talking Aline out of opening the ride if this lady was leaning over his shoulder while he was doing it. He took another cookie, crunched happily.

"She is not," Aunt Vera sniffed. "She is in town, having lunch with the president of the bank, if you please. I do not know what's going to become of that girl, acting like a regular business person. It is a shame and a scandal, and in my day it would never have been permitted."

Considering that the "day" Aunt Vera referred to was probably somewhere in the 1920s, she was probably right. Still, Sam felt compelled to defend the absent Aline. "I don't see why she can't do a good job running the park."

"Of course she could do a good job," Vera snapped back. "There's no question. But she shouldn't *have* to. That girl is past twenty-three and isn't married *yet*." She picked up a sugar cookie and crunched on it vindictively.

"Well, I'm sure she's had lots of chances," he said.

"Of course she has. She's a Schaeber. Never been a real man who didn't find a Schaeber woman attractive."

Belatedly, Sam noticed that Vera herself wasn't wearing a wedding ring. He took another cookie.

"Then she's probably just waiting for the right man to come along before she settles down," he said, mentally crossing his fingers. It was the expected thing to say, whether he believed it or not, and to come out with a 1990s attitude in the 1950s would only get him—he flinched away from the thought, too close for comfort even as a cliché.

There were only two cookies left on the plate. He glanced at them longingly, looked up to find Vera glaring. The message was clear—no more cookies. He put the envelope on the table and got up.

"Thank you for the lemonade and cookies, Miss Vera." His foot was asleep, and he winced as he put weight on it. "If you'll just make sure Ms. Schaeber gets this—"

Vera took the envelope. "The receipts, I suppose. Seems like you never come to visit anymore unless you've got somebody's receipts. It is a sin and a shame, Bob Watkins, the way things have changed around here." Her head bobbed in a decisive snap. "All right. I suppose you want a marker. Whose receipts are these?"

"Dusty's."

"All right." Vera left him standing in the kitchen and went into the next room. A few minutes later she came out again and tucked a piece of paper into his hand. "You take care of yourself, Bob Watkins. Don't you be so much a stranger, you hear? I for one don't believe a single word of those things they say about you. The only reason you talk to yourself is because you were sick, that's the only reason."

That, and a hologram who appeared to have gone on vacation, he amended mentally. But he smiled and extended his hand and left the house again, his stomach growling. The cookies weren't enough, and he needed something besides that awful lemonade.

He was some distance down the street when Al reappeared.

"Hey, you're still limping." The Observer was dressed now in a fairly conservative—a comparatively conservative—purple suit with a white and purple shirt and reverse-pattern tie. "Did you get kicked or something?"

"No, I didn't get kicked."

"Touchy, touchy. I take it you didn't talk her out of it, since you haven't Leaped." Al kept on walking beside him, even when it meant he "walked" right through a tree.

Sam stopped and stared at him. "Wait a minute."

"What?" Al looked around wildly. "What?"

"You've been beside me for most of a block now."

"Yeah, so?"

"So I want to know, just how big *is* this Imaging Chamber anyway?"

Al's gaze immediately became shifty, the way it always did when he didn't want to answer a question. "I can't tell you that, you know that. Ziggy says . . ."

"Oh, come on, what does what Ziggy says have to do with the dimensions of a room?" Sam was waving his arms for emphasis. Abruptly he noticed an elderly man sitting on a porch swing, and converted the gesture into a wave of greeting, smiling sheepishly. Through his teeth, he went on, "Well? How big? You're supposed to be standing there, your real body. So how can you walk this far without bumping into a wall?"

It didn't make sense that Al could keep walking beside him, and suddenly it annoyed the hell out of him. Al wouldn't tell him enough about himself. There were rules, he'd said once, rules Sam never remembered having made, that said he mustn't be told, he had to find out for himself. It must have something to do with changing the past too much, he had finally figured out. But he still wanted to know.

And knowing the size of the Imaging Chamber couldn't possibly affect what he did in the past.

Al shook his head. "It doesn't matter, Sam."

"It matters to me!"

And it did. Every time he Leaped he was starting over. He didn't even always have all the memories he'd had in the last Leap. So each time he was a stranger and afraid, in a world each time unmade. . . . He thought he remembered hating poetry.

"It's a big room," Al said reluctantly. "The Imaging Chamber has room for all kinds of people. Look, can we change the subject?"

"Yeah," Sam said, discouraged suddenly. "Never mind. Must be low blood sugar. I need to get something to eat. That whiskey, and that lemonade—" His face scrinched at the memory.

"Whiskey? Lemonade?" Al fell in step with him again, casting a wary glance at the handlink as he did so. "What did I miss?"

"Not much. I never even got to talk to Aline."
The explanation, and the description of Aunt
Vera, took them all the way back to the gates
of the park.

"You didn't?"

"She wasn't there."

"Oh." Al clenched the cigar between his teeth.
"Well, you're just going to have to keep trying,
then."

Sam dug into his—Bob's—jeans pocket and
found the couple of dollars that had been lying
on the dresser that morning. "Look, later, okay?
Right now I'm going to go get something to eat.
Why don't you try again to get some more information from Ziggy?"

Al started to say something, hesitated, and
took another look at him. He could see the wea-
riness that sometimes threatened to overwhelm
his friend in the subtle lines around his eyes—
Bob's eyes. "Sure, okay, Sam. No problem. I'll
be back with you later, okay?"

"Yeah, fine." Sam turned away, barely hearing the Door slide open.

"Sam—" Al started to say more, looking at
the other man's back. When Sam didn't move,
he finished lamely, "Take care of yourself, all
right?"

One hand waved him away impatiently. Closing his eyes and shaking his head, Al stepped
through the Door, leaving Sam behind again.

Sam listened to the sound of the Door closing
and shook his head as well. The only thing he

104

could accomplish right now was feeding Bob's body before it collapsed from hypoglycemia. That, at least, he could succeed in. He headed for one of the food stands operated by a vendor who'd seemed friendly the day before.

The booth sold hot dogs, hamburgers, caramel apples, and cotton candy. The vendor refused to take his money, but invited him inside, instead. "Oh no, Bob, you never pay. Besides, I want you to look at this machine. It doesn't work right."

"I'd be careful about that, Miguel. Things go a little caca around Bob, y'know." It was McFarland, pausing by the order window. He had a tool belt slung low around his hips, a grin on his face. His sandy hair was sticking up in all directions.

"You tried, Mr. McFarland. It is only fair to let Bob have his turn." Miguel's reply was cutting in its dignity.

"Suit yourself." McFarland sauntered away, toward the Ferris wheel, his hands in his pockets.

"You see here where the syrup comes in," Miguel was explaining. "It is supposed to go around and around and spin the sugar. It is not doing this."

The vendor shoved the machine around, away from the back of the little food stand, and the scent of hot dogs and popcorn filled Sam's nostrils, and he had to swallow the sudden rush of saliva. He might have been hungrier sometime, but he couldn't recall when. It was hard to concentrate on what Miguel was saying.

Sam could see the wad of blue cotton candy at the base of the rotating arm, and the drips of syrup. What he could not see was what was wrong with the machine. What he could remember about fixing anything at all, however, involved unplugging it first. Moving Miguel back out of the way, he bent over, looking for the power cord, and caught a glimpse of "himself" reflected in the protective glass of the machine. He blinked.

He could see—Bob Watkins, younger than Sam Beckett, dark hair, anxious blue eyes, freckles, the red in the plaid shirt clashing with the incipient sunburn. He could see Bob—

—with blue cotton candy in his hair, odd highlights glinting in his hair and clothes, and blood running down a cut in his cheek—

—and the machine shifted, as if jarred off a support of some kind, and turned on with a roar, and the glass blew out with a crack like thunder, spraying wickedly lethal shards in all directions.

Miguel yelled something as Sam threw up an arm to protect his, or Bob's, eyes, and the spinning arms whirled, sending wisps and clouds and gobs of blue cotton candy all over the booth, all over Miguel, all over Sam, and he could feel the warm trickle of blood sliding down his face, and hear Mike McFarland laughing.

CHAPTER
EIGHT

Aline Schaeber peeled off her white gloves and laid them across the latch of her patent-leather purse, hoping that Matt Jenkins couldn't see her hands trembling.

So many times she had heard Uncle Karl boast that he could walk into Jenkins' office and get a loan for any amount of money, any time, on nothing more than his word and a handshake. It was a mysterious matter of men and cigars and honor, he had implied, and she would never need to worry her pretty little head about it because he would always be there to take care of her and Vera.

The last time she'd been in this office was two months ago, for the reading of Karl's will. She'd been more concerned with supporting Vera, near collapse behind her black veil, than in paying any attention to the room itself. She'd been close to collapse herself, and there were so many people around, and then the will had been read and there seemed to be so much explaining to do to all the people who expected it to be different. Blinking, she shook the memory away quickly.

Now, waiting for Mr. Jenkins—Vera always called him "the president of the bank" or "Banker Jenkins," with a funny little twist to her mouth—in his office, she looked around, curious. The room was dominated by the biggest, glossiest oak desk she had ever seen, with a green felt blotter. He must not write very much, she thought. The pen nib would go right through the paper.

She folded her hands over her purse. It didn't feel right. She put the purse on the floor beside her feet and laid her hands primly in her lap. *Sit up straight, feet flat on the floor. Be a lady.*

Her hands didn't want to remain prim. Picking up the purse again, she recovered the gloves, opened the purse and put them inside.

A moment later she took the gloves out and pulled them on again.

Behind the desk was a huge mahogany leather chair, tufted with brass buttons. The armrests were shiny with years of wear. She thought about getting up to see if the chair had four feet or swiveled, but if she did, and Jenkins came in, she would be mortified. Sneaking around a banker's office was not the sort of thing a lady did.

But a lady could get up to examine the painting on the wall behind the chair, surely?

The chair had four solid feet. Years of moving the heavy chair back and forth had created permanent gouges in the wide-paneled floor.

And the oil painting, of a giant bull chewing a contemplative cud against a background of oil derricks and the silhouette of a city skyline. All about Oklahoma, she thought, smiling. Cattle and oil and cities.

And amusement parks, she reminded herself.

Vera was furious when she'd told her about coming to the bank. If she'd known about the bill in Aline's purse she would have had a conniption fit. Seven *thousand* dollars . . .

She returned to the chair on the other side of the desk, a smaller black leather chair with not nearly as many brass buttons, and sat down again to look at the paneling and wallpaper and peel the gloves off again, stuffing them in beside the bill.

She *had* to pay that bill.

And not even the best opening in the world would pay both Mike McFarland and all the other bills that she'd been so bravely promising would all be paid in full, as soon as the Killer Diller opened. She'd seen some of the vendors putting food back on the shelves in Talbot's grocery because they couldn't afford it, and it shamed her.

The door swung open, and Banker Jenkins came in. She popped to her feet before she could think, and then wavered, unable to decide whether she should sit down again and offer her hand or simply remain standing. Before she could decide he had come over to her and hugged her.

Jenkins was a big man with a wide, florid waistcoat and an old-fashioned watch chain. Fashionable folk in New York might be wearing single-breasted suits and pleatless pants, but Matt Jenkins was the President of the First (and only) Bank of Jasmine, Oklahoma, and fashions for bankers were what he said they were. His face was ruddy and he wheezed with the exertion of walking across the room. Long strands of hair were combed sideways across a shiny pate. He smelled of cigars and cologne.

"Aline Schaeber, aren't you just the prettiest thing! I am so sorry I kept you waiting here. But you know how business is," he chuckled. His voice was pitched high, so that if she closed her eyes she might mistake it for a child's. "I am just so pleased to see you. It's been—" Abruptly he remembered how long it had been, and under what circumstances she'd last been there, and changed the subject. "Now, to what do I owe this great pleasure?"

"Ban—er," she cleared her throat and started over, "Mr. Jenkins, I've come to talk to you about a loan."

"A loan? Well, good heavens, child, you didn't need to come down here for that. You know I'm happy to help you out anytime you want."

Aline's immediate surge of relief was followed by an uncomfortable feeling that when Jenkins said "child," he meant it. He wasn't thinking in terms of a bank loan; he was thinking in terms of a nickel for cotton candy.

"A business loan, Mr. Jenkins. For Family World."

The warmth in the room cooled perceptibly, and his merry blue eyes narrowed. "A business loan? Well, well, well."

She was still standing, and didn't know whether she should sit down or not. Jenkins circled the desk, looked at his appointment calendar, pulled out his watch and flipped open the cover.

"I really need a loan," she said. It was not what she'd meant to say. It was not the tone she'd meant to use.

"Well, now," Jenkins said. "A business loan. Hmmmm." He looked at his watch again.."Well, now. That's a very serious thing, a business loan."

"I know," she said, hating the feeling of helplessness, of wanting Karl to be here and take over. "I need eight thousand dollars."

Jenkins blinked. Aline twisted her hands.

"I suggest that we go and have ourselves a late lunch. I haven't eaten yet and I'm feeling a mite peckish. And we can talk about this loan that

111

you need." Nodding decisively, he came around the desk again and took her by the arm to lead her out of the office.

She wanted to tell him no, that she wanted to conduct a business discussion in a business setting, but by that time they were going past the secretary and he was telling her that he would be taking Miss Schaeber to eat at Winston's and he'd be back about four, thank you kindly.

Winston's was the place that Karl used to take her for her birthday. It was by far the nicest place in Jasmine, with linen tableclothes and heavy sterling service, with cut crystal water and wine glasses and vases with a single daisy for a centerpiece at each table. It was a wonderful place, filled with wonderful memories, and it wasn't where Aline wanted to have a business meeting.

The waiter brought menus, huge oversized things with ornate gold printing. Vera had always said a lady ordered from the mid-range of the menu, but there were no prices on Aline's.

On the other hand she wasn't sure she could keep anything down anyway.

"The steak is good," Jenkins rumbled.

"I think I'd like the trout," she said. Jenkins raised an eyebrow. "But I'll have the steak," she amended hastily. "The steak sounds wonderful."

The waiter responded to an invisible signal. "The lady will have the trout, with a small glass of white wine," Jenkins said. "And I'll have your big steak. Well done." He slapped the menu closed, and the waiter collected them, bowing as he left them.

Aline stared at the tablecloth, her face red.

"Now that's your first lesson," Jenkins said. "Decide what you want and stick to your guns. You want the trout, you say so, and you stick to it. Understand?"

She wasn't sure she did, but she nodded anyway.

The salads came, and she carved the cherry tomatoes in half and ate, feeling a wash of relief. This much she was secure in; she knew how to behave in a nice restaurant. Karl and Vera had made sure of it. Jenkins made small talk about the weather and mutual acquaintances— at least, acquaintances of Karl Schaeber's and Matt Jenkins'—and church activities, and said hello to others coming into Winston's for lunch. She drank less than a third of her glass of wine, and thought she detected a glint of approval in the banker's eyes.

By the time the waiter came by with the dessert menu, she was feeling much more secure about herself. She was being treated like a lady, not like a petitioner.

Then Matt Jenkins rose and escorted her back to his office, and suddenly she was a petitioner again. But at least she was a fed petitioner this time, and she had the recent sensation of wide respect and admiration to support her when she sank back into the black leather chair.

Jenkins plopped himself into the big chair and scraped it forward, no doubt adding to the gouges in the wood, and laced his fingers together, resting his hands on the blotter.

"First off, I want to thank you for your company today, Miss Schaeber. It was very kind of you to accompany an old man. Makes him feel young again."

She smiled uncertainly, picking up the signal in the changed form of address but not sure exactly what it meant. "Now, you said you needed a business loan for Family World. I believe you mentioned eight thousand dollars."

"Yes, sir, Mr. Jenkins."

"For Family World." When she nodded, he said, "I see."

There was a long pause, during which Aline desperately wanted to pull on her gloves again to hide the sweat she could feel on her palms.

"And what exactly is the bank's money going to be used for?" he said.

"Bills. The new ride. I—I didn't realize the bill for the ride hadn't been paid. When Uncle Karl died, everything was confused. That's why we had to delay opening—you know we originally planned to open on the Fourth of July. But this bill slipped through, and I need the money to pay it." She tried to sound matter-of-fact about it. She had been up half the night, trying to project how much the opening would bring in. She had bought advertisements on the radio, and they'd sounded exciting even to her when she heard them. Roller coasters were supposed to bring in people from two hundred miles around, and people were supposed to ride it again and again for the thrill. But she didn't know if they would.

Jenkins' eyebrows were arched very high. "Eight thousand dollars. My, my. That's quite a lot of money."

She swallowed. "I know it is. But that's how much I need." It would cover McFarland's bill, and tomorrow's paychecks, and the most pressing bills. At fifty cents apiece admission, she would have to bring in sixteen thousand people over the weekend if she was going to be able to pay it back all at once.

They hadn't even had sixteen thousand people at the Fourth of July picnic. She wasn't sure there were sixteen thousand people in this part of Oklahoma. At least, not sixteen thousand with money to go to an amusement park. But then there was the quarter per person per ride—if each person rode it twice, she'd only need eight thousand. And they didn't all have to show up this one weekend.

And you didn't have to pay back loans right away.

"I could get by—no. I need eight. Thousand. Dollars. By tomorrow."

He shook his head. "That is a devil of a lot of money, Aline."

"I know it." She took her courage and her purse in both hands, and she could hear McFarland's bill rustling. "I know it is, but that's what it will take. And I can pay it back. I have the projected income. When the ride opens, I'll have it back."

"And pay the bank back."

"Schaebers have never failed to pay their debts," she said proudly. She didn't know, in fact, if Karl had ever failed or not, but she had heard him say it often enough. "Our word is our bond."

"Well, that's certainly been my experience, I must say it has." Jenkins picked up a fountain pen and turned it end-to-end in his stubby fingers. "Eight thousand. I can't authorize a loan of that size without the agreement of the Board of Directors."

"My Uncle Karl always said the Board of Directors did exactly what you wanted them to do." The words surprised her. Her own daring surprised her.

It surprised him, too, and pleased him. He laughed, a high-pitched giggle. "Your Uncle Karl gave me a lot of credit."

"It's true, isn't it?"

Jenkins' fingers on the fountain pen tightened suddenly. "How is your Aunt Vera, girl?"

"My what?" This change in subject she was totally unprepared for. "My Aunt Vera? She's fine."

"Wonderful woman, your Aunt Vera." He laid the pen down on the blotter, squaring it carefully with the edge. "Just a wonderful woman." He looked up again and met her anxious gaze. "Now, for all the credit your Uncle Karl gave me, the truth of the matter is that the Board listens to me, all right. But the Bank Examiners look very closely at transactions the size of this one."

But what does Aunt Vera have to do with it? she almost said. She couldn't make a connection between Jenkins' influence with the Board and Aunt Vera's health, and Jenkins was obviously not going to make it for her. Aunt Vera had despised the man for as long as she could remember.

"I don't understand," she said at last.

"I can't make a loan this size without some kind of collateral," he said. "The Bank Examiners won't let me. They look out for our stockholders, and they want us to have collateral. Do you know what collateral is, Aline?"

"Of course I know," she said indignantly, her heart sinking. "I'm not stupid, Mr. Jenkins." Perhaps Karl Schaeber *could* get a loan on no more than the strength of his word, but the fact was that he hadn't. And the option wasn't going to be offered to Aline Schaeber.

"I never said you were. Schaeber women aren't. That's a lesson I learned a long time ago." The pudgy man across the desk from her smiled quickly, then became serious. "Do you know

117

about the mortgage on the park?"

"I've been making payments on it for three months."

"Then you understand that I can't give you any more on it. What else do you have that you can offer, Aline? What do the Schaebers have that's worth eight thousand dollars?"

CHAPTER
NINE

By the time he walked away from the booth, coated with dirt and glass, bits of blue cotton candy still drifting from his hair, it was close to sunset, and Sam still hadn't eaten. Miguel was still shouting after him. It was pure luck that nobody had been seriously hurt. McFarland had raced back to disconnect the machine gone berserk before it set fire to the whole line of booths, and had defended him to the furious Miguel.

Granted, the defense had been rife with words like "amateur handymen," "just plain unlucky," and "I told you I'd fix the thing tomorrow, Miguel, you didn't need to be in such a dad-blamed hurry." McFarland handed Sam a broom to clean up with while he more or less calmed down Miguel, Miguel's wife, and Miguel's three kids. Then he extracted something charred and sticky from the guts of the machine, stripped wires, taped things, and wrenched things around. In general, he gave a marvelously efficient performance, while Sam tried to keep the floor from crunching under the other man's efficient feet.

Sam hunched his shoulders against Miguel's last few comments and made his way past the visitors finally arriving as the evening cooled, past the office and back to the cluster of trailers. With a sigh of relief he closed the door of his trailer behind himself and slumped against it.

Threads of spun sugar floated past his nose, and he stuck out his lower lip and blew upward. The effort only attached them to his eyebrows. Muttering to himself, he scraped at his face and began peeling off his sticky clothes.

Finishing his shower, he peered into the mirror, rubbing his face, trying to decide if he needed a shave. He decided that it would be beside the point. Bob looked like the kind of guy who had some trouble raising a beard, and nobody except Al—and children, and animals—would ever see anyone but Bob. Sam Beckett could grow a full beard, and who would know? Dr. Beeks, maybe? Thirty or forty years in the future? His hair could be dyed pink and nobody would ever know. He could—

He could go get some dinner, that's what he could do. He got dressed, found some more money tucked in the back of Bob's sock drawer, and went into town.

He found a diner with a booth in the back, ordered a "Hometown Special: meat loaf, green beans, mashed potatoes with Mom's Own Gravy!" and pushed the silverware around until it came.

It wasn't bad, though Mom's Own Gravy could have used a little less salt. He ordered a second helping of plum pie and poked at the crust aimlessly. The heavy, useless sensation of physical depression was rapidly fading. The general malaise of spirit was still present.

"Now that looks like a *damn* fine cup of coffee," Al said, popping in beside him. "Now that you've eaten, are you human again?"

"Yeah, I guess." Sam pulled in a deep breath. "Yeah. Okay. What does Ziggy have to say?"

"Not much yet."

"Why do I have this feeling that there's something you're not telling me again?"

"It's nothing, just a little glitch, we're getting it worked out. Did you talk to Aline?"

"No, I didn't talk to Aline." Al, taken aback at his tone, flinched. Sam relented. "She wasn't there. I told you that hours ago."

Willing to be mollified, Al said, "I *know* that. I just thought maybe you went back later, while I was gone."

"No." Sam shoved the pie plate away.

121

Al eyed the remains of the plum pie longingly. "So what happened?"

"Nothing."

Sam's tone caught Al's full attention. He cocked a beady eye at the other man, who still had a laden fork in his hand. "Oh. Nothing. Right."

"I'm just tired, okay? I want to get this Leap over with, that's all. Give me a break, Al."

Get this Leap over with, and go on to the next Leap. It hung unspoken in the air between man and hologram.

"Do you suppose you could eat that bite of pie instead of just sitting there tantalizing me with it?" Al said at last. "Even if you're tired you can still chew."

Sam shrugged. "Not hungry anymore." He replaced the fork on the plate, rested one fist on top of another and his chin on top of both.

For the space of a number of long breaths Al studied him. The lights of the handlink flickered between them, painting Al's face and hands in yellow and pink and green and blue. The only light touching Sam's came from the white bulb in the café's ceiling light.

The strain was beginning to catch up, Al thought. On all of them. He wouldn't have said whatever it was he said to Tina, if he wasn't under such strain all the time, finding Sam each time he Leaped, unable to provide any help but words. Tina wouldn't have been so mad if he hadn't kept after her all the time about making sure Ziggy was always in top operating condition. Dr. Beeks could use a rest from greeting a different stranger in Sam's body, trying to get information out of people who were terrified and out of their minds—out of their bodies, anyway—quite literally, telling them they weren't crazy, they weren't kidnapped by aliens, they weren't anything at all. Of course, Beeks couldn't tell them where they *were*, either. Most of them wouldn't handle the news that they were in somebody else's body in the future at all well.

And Sam was just tired of Leaping.

"Hey," Al said quietly. "Remember Jimmy LaMotta? The special kid you Leaped into? He's doing great. He worked on the docks for three years, and then got hired in an office. Now he's doing administrative stuff with Special Olympics."

Sam didn't respond.

"And Samantha Stormer? She's an executive at General Motors now."

Still no response.

"And Tibby Johnson is—"

"Quit it, Al." Sam didn't raise his head.

"He speaks!"

"I mean it, Al. I know what you're trying to do, and I appreciate it, but just cut it out, okay?"

"Okay." When Sam still didn't move, he heaved a sigh and went on, "Okay. Ziggy is still sorting through the data, but what we've got now is, the accident was no accident."

That got through. Sam raised his head, met Al's gaze. "What do you mean?"

"Just what I said. Ziggy says the probability is eighty-seven percent that the accident was no accident. It was deliberate."

"But you said seven people died." A growing bleakness in Sam's eyes indicated that he had grasped exactly what Al was saying; he was simply refusing to say it.

So Al said it for him. "They were murdered."

Aline Schaeber sat at the dining room table and stared at the sheaf of paper spread out before her. She had moved from the kitchen into the dining room because Vera was in the kitchen, rattling dishes angrily; here at least she could concentrate a little better.

To her right, a stack of envelopes teetered alarmingly, threatening to slide to the floor.

In front of her, an old-fashioned account book showed neat columns of entries in precise ink, most of it red.

To her left, a fan of bills. Insurance. Food. Fuel oil. Hay. More insurance. A list of employee wages, due and payable tomorrow.

And one other piece of paper folded in fourths. Mike McFarland's bill.

And in her hands, a loan application.

The loan application was for more money than she had ever seen in her life at one time.

She chewed on her lip, studied the application. If she closed her eyes she could recite the essential clauses from memory. The one about collateral was particularly vivid. She raised her head from the application and looked around the house, Vera's house, Karl's, filled with loving memories. It was such a terrible risk to take, staking this house on the success of a new attraction.

But was it such a risk, if she was right?

Vera came in with a glass of milk, set it on the table. Aline hastily folded the paper up again.

"Your Uncle Karl always did his business in the office," she sniffed. "He never brought it home, and he certainly never spread it all over the dining room table at suppertime."

"I'm sure he didn't, Aunt Vera." Aline's response was absentminded as she ran a fingernail down the last column of figures in the account book, trying to convey that she was busy, that she didn't have the time to talk. The polish on the nail was chipped around the edges, and Vera pursed her lips at the sight of it.

"Well then, I don't see why you have to." She sat down next to the younger woman. "I don't see why you have to bother about any of this."

Aline bit back an exasperated response. When she had her temper under control, she said, "I *want* to, Aunt Vera. More than anything else in my life I want to."

"It's unnatural."

"It is *not* unnatural."

"Don't you raise your voice to me, young lady. I raised you. I took care of you and Karl both."

"I know that, Aunt Vera."

"Then you listen to me. You get rid of this business and get yourself married like a decent woman."

"Aren't you a decent woman?"

"Katherine Aline Schaeber, what are you saying?" Vera lunged to her feet. "What do you think you're implying?"

Aline backed down. "Nothing, Aunt Vera. It's just that you've never been married, and I've always considered you the most decent, respectable woman I know. Everybody does. So I don't see why you think I have to be married to be decent."

But Vera was not to be placated. "Everybody in this town knows I was engaged to be married. Everybody! And I would be married this very day if Lhatt Stevens hadn't died in that well accident in Muskogee. And I take it as an insult for the likes of you, who I raised from the time you were three years old, to make fun of an old woman who . . ."

" . . . chose to remain true to the memory of her first great love," Aline chorused with her, "no matter what other offers she had . . ."

Vera stopped cold as she realized what had just happened. "I take it," she said, gathering the rags of her dignity around her, "that you have heard me say this before."

"Yes ma'am, I have."

"Then that makes it that much worse." Vera wrapped skinny arms across her bosom.

"Maybe I just haven't been so lucky as you," Aline said gently. "I haven't had a chance to find my first great love."

Vera's expression, but not her tone, softened. "And you certainly won't find it in those account books and bills. There hasn't been a woman yet found any love at all in an account book."

The back door rattled, and Vera got up to answer it. "I just want you to be happy, honey. I want you to have a family, have children. And it just won't happen while you're all wrapped up in business."

"I know, Aunt Vera," she said softly as the older woman left the room. *But this is more important right now*, she did not add.

It was Jesse, with more receipts. He came in and dumped them in a pile on the edge of the table, and Aline had to lunge to rescue them from sliding off. "Thank you, Jesse," she said brightly. "I surely do appreciate your bringing these by."

Jesse grunted, and bent over with bad grace to pick up some envelopes and invoices that had escaped. "Sight o' bills here," he said.

"Yes, there are." Aline held out her hand for the ones he had gathered.

Turning them over with bad grace, his eye fell on the folded loan application she had set to one side when Vera came in. "What's that?" he demanded, reaching for it.

She whisked it out from under his hand. "A business transaction," she said smoothly.

"Nothing you need to worry about, Jesse. Everything's under control."

Jesse's eyes blazed. "Nothing I need to worry about, hey? I suppose you know exactly what you're doing?"

"Yes, I do."

"They don't insure places like Family World against bankruptcy, you know," he snapped. "You'd better know what you're doing."

"I can handle it, Jesse, thank you."

In the doorway, Vera cleared her throat. Jesse looked around, and his shoulders slumped. "All right. All right, then. But if you need—I always used to do the books, after Karl got bad. I could help you out if you wanted."

"I appreciate that, Jesse, I surely do." Smiling, she got to her feet and guided him to Vera, who escorted him out.

She was sitting with her elbows on the table and her head in her hands when Vera came back, sliding into the chair as if there had been no interruption.

"Now you're getting headaches," Vera fretted. "I want you to put those things away right this minute, Katherine Aline. There are people better qualified than you are to make those decisions. Jesse . . ."

"No, I don't believe there are people better qualified. Not who care as much as I do." Raising her head, Aline took one of the pieces of paper half-hidden under the stack of invoices, clipped to one of them. She detached it from the bill and spread it out on the table between them. It was an advertisement, bright and bold with red and black and a picture of a giant roller coaster.

"This is it, Aunt Vera. This is going to make all the difference, and this is what Jesse doesn't understand. I've talked to people, men who own amusement parks like ours in other parts of the country, and they all agree that roller coasters are the most popular rides of all. They bring in more money. They bring in people who otherwise wouldn't come to an amusement park at all. You watch. Come Sunday, all this—" she waved her hand at the bills and envelopes and account books—"all this is going to change. We're going to turn a profit, make Schaeber's Family World bigger and better and more famous than it's ever been."

Her face was taut with the need to convince the other woman. Vera drew away, rejecting, but Aline went on, "It's what Uncle Karl wanted, what he always dreamed of. It's my dream too, has been ever since I was old enough to understand.

"Sunday, Aunt Vera. Success is that close. Only three days away! How can you ask me to walk away from it—from everything I know, from all my dreams—now? You know how important it is to have a dream! Isn't it even more important to have it come true?"

Vera picked up the glass and drained it herself as if it were water for a drowning man. "I don't think that you should walk away," she muttered reluctantly. "It just isn't ladylike, that's all."

"Lady is as lady does, you always taught me. And this is what this lady's going to do."

Unable to think of any more arguments, Vera picked up the empty glass and took it with her into the kitchen, a dissatisfied "Humph" hanging in the air behind her. Aline bit back a smile and bent to the account books again.

On Jesse Bartlett's sixteenth birthday, the stock market in New York City crashed, marking the beginning of the Great Depression. In one day his father went from being a wealthy man with stock in a dozen companies to being a pauper, unable to keep a roof over his family's head. After the only surviving bank in Jasmine took the home place, Dace Bartlett went out to the old cow barn with his favorite shotgun and blew his brains out.

Nobody had the money to buy the Bartlett place, and the president of the bank let Jesse and his mother and sisters stay, reminding them at least twice a week that they were there only on charity.

Jesse struggled while his mother mourned the tales of lost glory, hearing them told every night as bedtime tales, consuming them with the chicken the family had every day, twice a day—chickens raised for eggs and feathers. They only ate the eggs on Sunday: the rest of the time they were sold. The capons and hens too old to lay landed on their table, fried, baked, boiled, stewed, roasted.

When he got older, he refused to touch chicken anymore.

He learned early he had a knack for fixing things, coaxing mechanical things to work again. If you fixed them, you didn't have to spend money to buy new. If you saved, you could buy back things like a house, or land. Even if it took years. His sisters grew up and got married and moved away, and then there was just himself and his mother. He thought sometimes of having a family, but there was no time and no money for frivolous things like courtship.

With the war, there was more money. Most of the country got on its feet again. Farmers who didn't have to worry about coupons could sell eggs and make a profit. Jesse tried to sign up for the Army, but they gave him an exemption for weak eyes and sent him back to grow wheat. He went back, reluctantly, to the bank for a loan for seed.

He was better at fixing things. Three crops failed in a row. The bank came back for their money, and his mother died one winter afternoon, sitting in her rocking chair looking out the back window toward the old barn. Jesse looked around at what he could sell to stave off disaster.

Most of the land disappeared quickly. There was a place on the old maps of Oklahoma called Bartlett Corners, because Bartletts owned all four sides along the crossroad. There were stories handed down about the jars of gold and silver coins buried out behind the cow barn where Dace had died; some said he shot himself out of pure frustration, being unable to find what his daddy before him had hidden too well. There were stories about the Indian burial grounds; they were close enough to the tribal towns that some believed that, and said Dace had been terrified into shooting himself by a ghostly vision of the tattered survivors of the Trail of Tears making their way across the red dirt of the south forty. Jesse sometimes felt the stories were like a yoke of water buckets on his shoulders, and he staggered between them, pulled this way and that and unable to walk straight. His roots were in the land and would not let him go. Even though Bartlett Corners was now only a name on a map.

When the revival preachers came, he was glad to take their money to let them set up in the remaining fields. It gave him some cash money so he could hold his head up in town. It was a good deal.

And when Karl Schaeber came to him with a proposal for a little park with some rides for the kiddies that were born after the soldiers came home, that was a good deal too. It had felt good, being equal partners with a respected man like Karl Schaeber. But the soldiers who came home didn't stay long enough, and both Schaeber and he had struggled to keep the park going. Karl was in better financial shape to begin with, and had quietly bought out Jesse's interest to keep the bank at bay. Never once had Karl treated Jesse like an employee, not even when the park expanded with the Schaeber name on it. Never once, until the lawyers read the will.

Now even the south forty belonged to someone else, and was covered over with asphalt paving and neon signs.

He tapped an unfiltered cigarette out of a worn leather case and lit it, taking a deep drag. He allowed himself twenty per day, no more, no less, and savored each one. He would not look at the books again until he was finished.

It should have been Bartlett's, not Schaeber's, Family World. Karl had promised him. Those Schaebers never could keep their promises. He could see it now with Aline. She talked all sweet, sure, but she was going to get rid of him. He could tell. She had that same look in her eye that Karl used to get when he looked at the park. Pride and possession, that was it. Pride and possession.

He watched the sun going down, the lights coming up. Lightning bugs began to dance in the dusk, and the children came out to chase them, trap them in jars and try to stay awake all night watching them. The end of his cigarette glowed in rhythm with the flickering of the insects.

The smoke burned his throat and lungs, and he coughed, clearing the phlegm out of his system. It happened more often lately. He didn't notice.

He smoked the cigarette down to a stub, crushed it out on the broad painted boards of the porch. His break over, he shoved himself out of the porch chair and returned to the office in the back of the little house.

His mother had told him about the wonderful house she grew up in, reminded him of the house they'd lived in before the Crash. This house, the one he lived in now, had been paid for by Schaeber money, earned by Jesse Bartlett working at Schaeber's Family World, built on Bartlett land. The books showed a steady flow of money going out. They covered the last three years, years during which Karl Schaeber had steadily declined and Jesse Bartlett had steadily taken greater control of the park.

It had been his great opportunity, and he had made the least of it. Even he could see it, in retrospect: the bad decisions, the gambles not taken. But at the time they had always seemed to be the right decisions. And he *was* damned good at fixing things. It had come as a shock when Judge Grant read the will and he found out that Karl had left it all to the girl. It wasn't right.

And then she didn't do the right thing and give it to him and let him fix it. She ran it herself. Kept him working, of course. "Valued his experience," she said.

That was the worst thing about this Killer Diller. It was Karl's idea originally. He'd made the contract. But when he died and Aline took over, even though she knew that Jesse was good at fixing things, she kept on a stranger anyway, a man from outside, somebody nobody'd ever heard of to set up and maintain Karl's bright new idea. She'd kept on that Mike McFarland, who talked so fast nobody could understand him and laughed at the way a regular person expressed himself.

Jesse cleared his throat, hawked the phlegm into a handkerchief.

McFarland directed the construction of the roller coaster, giving Jesse orders as if he, Jesse Bartlett, were some kind of a field hand. Cost a sight o' money, too, if the books were right. And they'd had to move folks around who'd had booths in those spots for a dozen years, just so he could site his ride in just the right place, overlooking Milsom's Pond. Didn't care in the least about those folks.

And the advertising! Bartletts had always believed that people would hear about you if you were good enough. And Karl had agreed. Why, how many times had he sat out on that very porch with the fat old man and watched the people come through that front gate, spend their money on rides and laughter? Never had to advertise.

But now, he had in front of him a flyer with a picture and big letters, no better than a drugstore having a sale. Selling fear, it looked like. "KILLER DILLER," it said. And in letters a little bit smaller, "The Thrill of a Lifetime!", winding up and down along the tracks in the picture. Copies of this flyer had been pasted up in every store in Jasmine, in every little town for forty miles. Aline had made a determined effort to advertise the Killer Diller.

And Jesse knew how she was paying for it all. Just like Karl, she'd gone to the banks, against his best advice, his warnings. That was one part of his experience she hadn't valued at all, to stay away from the damned banks. The account books were dismal, reflecting a load of debt that made his gut churn. She just wouldn't listen.

But the flyer—even he could feel a stir of excitement at the thought of sitting in a car that climbed, and climbed, seventy feet in the air, and then dropped almost straight down, up again, and around and around and up and down. It must be the way the birds felt, that ride.

He reached for the worn leather cigarette case again, realized what he was doing and put it away. He'd had his last cigarette for the day; he wouldn't allow himself to have another. But the lighter was still in his hand, and with the other he crumpled the flyer into a sudden tight ball and lit it, tossing it to the floor like a giant firefly tail.

At least she'd bought insurance. That might come in handy. That might save them from that terrible load of debt.

It should have been his. He was *good* at fixing things.

Friday

CHAPTER
TEN

Admiral Al Calavicci woke up in his quarters at Project Quantum Leap, rolled out of bed and looked at the terminal humming quietly on the desk across the room. There were no messages. He rubbed his eyes and swore.

Personnel quarters at the Project were not elaborate. Like everyone else associated with Quantum Leap, he had a single room and a utilitarian bathroom. Unlike many of the others, he had almost nothing in the way of personal decoration. The time spent in the Navy, the requirements of numerous alimony payments, and personal preference all kept his room to Spartan standards. The two framed pictures on the wall were photographs from the Gallup Intertribal Indian Ceremonials, available by mail order from a dozen suppliers. The desk held nothing but the remote terminal, one of Ziggy's dumber relatives. The bed had plain sheets and rumpled Army olive-drab blankets. There was a telephone on the table at the other end of the room. A shelf over the desk supported engineering textbooks and a well-thumbed dictionary.

The room might have been occupied by anybody. It held no personality at all. Al Calavicci traveled light and fast, he often said. His friends thought sometimes he slowed down a little too often—hence the alimony payments.

Calavicci padded to the bathroom, preparing for another day, another battle, another morning shower and shave. Toweling himself dry when he came out, he checked the terminal again. Nothing had changed. He tapped at the keyboard, frustrated.

YES, ADMIRAL? The response on the screen was immediate.

What information do you have on the accident? he typed.

EVIDENCE INDICATES THAT THE INCIDENT WAS DELIBERATELY ENGINEERED.

He ground his teeth in frustration. Ziggy might be smarter than any other computer on earth, but he was still too damned literal-minded. Al wasn't sure that was because Ziggy was a computer, or because he was built with input from Sam Beckett. *What further information is available*?

UNABLE TO ACCESS. The terminal paused, flickered. SORRY, ADMIRAL.

"Ah, shit." Al finished drying himself and hung the towel neatly over a towel bar. His routine in the morning was fixed, had been since the days when he was a POW in Vietnam and his sanity depended on it, and it always included forty-five minutes of intense exercise. When he finished, he was not breathing particularly hard. He ducked back in the shower again to rinse the sweat away. Five years without the chance to take a bath had also left him with a mania for personal cleanliness. Rubbing himself down briskly, he burrowed through the wardrobe that took up one corner of the room.

The open door of the wardrobe revealed the only note of color in the room. There were several notes of color, in fact, purples and reds and greens clashing with each other, and off in a corner, under blue dry-cleaning plastic, two sets of dress whites. All the extravagance that was missing from Al's living quarters showed up in his closet, with a vengeance.

Al himself thought that the room was the best reflection of himself that there was. He did not, when he thought this, consider the room barren.

Dressed, finally, in a green suit with darker green suspenders, a pale yellow shirt—the resemblance to a daisy was quite amazing—he left the room without locking it and headed for the Operations Center.

Project Quantum Leap was buried in a remote corner of New Mexico, in land so desolate that it took fifty acres to support one cow or two jackrabbits. There were few roads; there weren't even any commercial flight corridors crossing over it. It was, the government had decided, an excellent spot to perform experiments, especially experiments that they weren't quite certain about. They could afford, they felt, to indulge their brightest scientist in an opportunity to do pure research on the nature of time, so long as everyone understood that the opportunity wasn't open-ended. They'd want results. Until they got results, the Project was to be kept top secret. Nightmares of *National Enquirer* headlines about what was going on gave congressional staffers cold chills.

As usual, the fact that getting results and doing pure research were two totally different things escaped Congress entirely. Nonetheless, Sam had talked them into funding the Project, and taken Al along. So the remote site was as much of a home as Al had. And he, and the couple of hundred other people involved in putting the Project together, had made it as livable as possible, given the constraints of secrecy.

The Operations Center was deep within an artificial cave system. To get to it, he had to leave the living quarters, enter another building, and take an elevator down to the weather tunnels, drilled not only to hide the extent of the complex but also to allow people to go back and forth even when snow or lightning made going even a dozen yards as much as one's life was worth. The tunnels were chilly, but at least they weren't windy. When the New Mexico winds kicked up, carrying sand or rain or ice, they could strip paint off a truck or blind the unwary.

There were a few engineers and maintenance people around to return his greetings, but for the most part he walked alone, his footsteps muffled by the unfinished concrete floors. The fluorescent lighting cast strange shadows against the raw walls around him as he went. Al always expected to find snakes in the tunnels, or have a bat swoop down and tangle itself in his hair. It hadn't happened yet, but that didn't mean it wouldn't. He kept a sharp eye out, and breathed an unconscious sigh of relief when he arrived in the working center of the Project.

As always, he stopped first in the Waiting Room. He waved to the nurse, one of Dr. Beeks' assistants, on duty in the observation bay, and walked over to the body in the hospital bed. Sam had been shaved that morning, and his cheeks were still red in places.

He made himself look, recognize the visitor occupying Sam's body. "We're trying our best to get you out of here, kiddo. We're trying our best to get you home."

Ritual complete, he glanced upward again. The nurse nodded and stuck a thumb up, indicating that for the time being, catatonic or not, the body in the bed was still healthy. The people who found themselves in the Waiting Room were not always catatonic. They

143

kept the body in good condition. Al sometimes thought of it in terms of a phrase of
Edgar Cayce's, "We have the body." They
certainly did, and it was damned frustrating.

The next stop after the Waiting Room was the
central Control Room. Gushie was still under
the table, as if he had never gone to bed; the
chances were good that he hadn't. Ominously,
more of the colored blocks had gone dark.

"Ziggy?" he called out, looking up and around.

"Admiral." The voice that answered him
was not the expected even baritone. Normally
Ziggy's tone was not only calm but smug. Now
it was shrill and anxious. Al glanced at Gushie.
The loss of the lights indicated that Ziggy was
steadily losing ground.

"Ziggy, have you located Tina?"

"No, sir."

Ziggy was definitely sick. The computer was
not given to granting honorifics to anyone but
its creator, and not often then.

"Why not, dammit?" It was an unreasonable
question and he knew it, but as he watched,
another set of lights flickered. If the lights went
out—if Ziggy's critical paths were reduced too
much—they would forever lose the ability to
home in on Sam.

If they did that, they would be unable to help
him prevent the derailing of the roller coaster. If
he failed to change history, he would be trapped
in it, unable to Leap onward.

And according to Ziggy's last review of what happened, he would be committed to an asylum, whereupon he really would go mad, and die. His body in the Waiting Room, occupied by a stranger, might continue to live, but it wouldn't be Sam Beckett.

He would be lost forever, unless the merciless unknown power that triggered the original malfunction in the Accelerator, causing him to Leap to begin with, relented.

Admiral Calavicci was not prepared to let chance define his battles.

Even if his own mistakes caused the battles to begin with.

"I am monitoring credit card transactions and activity on Dr. Martinez-O'Farrell's bank account," the computer responded. "There has been no sign."

"Then she must be visiting family, or a girl-friend somewhere. Check the known associates listed on her Personnel Security Questionnaire."

"That would be in violation of the Privacy Act."

"I don't care," Al said through clenched teeth. "Do it!" One did not get to be an admiral without learning how to give orders.

"*Working*," the computer responded reluctantly. "But I will be unable to continue processing 1957 information while doing so."

From underneath the table, Gushie cursed.

"Gushie, have you had any sleep? Anything to eat?"

"Uh, yes sir."

"Gushie last slept twenty-seven hours ago," the computer interrupted. "His last meal was primarily fats and refined sugars, sixteen hours ago."

Al crouched down to peer under the table. Sure enough, beside the programmer the crumpled remains of a candy bar wrapper backed up Ziggy's talebearing.

"Ziggy, go do what you were told. Gushie, go to bed. That's an order."

"But sir—" Gushie wiggled out from under the table and faced the other man almost nose-to-nose. Well, not quite; it was closer to nose-to-forehead, Al being a few essential inches shorter. Al backed away. It wasn't Gushie's fault he had bad breath, not entirely; it didn't have to be quite so bad, though.

Al rarely gave a thought to the effect his incessant cigar smoking had on his own breath.

"Sir," Gushie went on, "I've almost got it, I'm sure—" The chief programmer for the Project had a high-pitched, rapid laugh, a round face divided by a thin mustache, and sweaty palms. As Sam had once observed, you couldn't make Gushie mad, but you could anxious him a lot. His nails were always nibbled down to nothing.

"Gushie has made several errors in the last three hours," Ziggy noted.

"Ziggy, dammit, mind your own business," Al said, annoyed at the interruption.

"I am capable of multitasking on this level." The computer sounded insulted.

"I don't care how many tasks you can handle, right now I want you to locate Tina, not make snide comments about Gushie." Al felt like he was mediating between a pair of six-year-olds on a playground.

Ziggy made a sound very like a snort, but kept its peace.

"Thank you, sir," Gushie said humbly.

Al sighed. It had been so much easier when Sam was running things. Somehow Sam could keep Ziggy in line and make Gushie feel less persecuted by the computer he was trying to program, create new paths in fuzzy logic, and keep the team working smoothly, so that all Al had to do was Project administration and hunt for funds. They divided the Project between them in an amazingly efficient fashion. Now Al had to do it by himself, and he often thought he'd rather be back on an aircraft carrier, even if he did have to be celibate.

Except that if he did, of course, Sam would be lost. And that was *not* going to happen.

"You have your orders, mister. And so do you," he said to the air. "I'm going to the Imaging Chamber."

"I will be unable to home you in on Dr. Beckett while executing the search parameters."

Al flinched. It hadn't occurred to him that Ziggy wouldn't even be able to send him to his friend. The situation must be even worse than he thought.

"How long will it take to execute search parameters?"

"Estimate forty-seven point three minutes from . . . Mark."

"Fine," he said decisively. "I'll go get something to eat. *Then* I'll . . . see what happens next."

Sam Beckett, for his part, awoke knowing it was Friday, July 12, 1957, and hot. This morning, at least, he knew where to get breakfast. Bob was running out of money, but with luck, this was payday. He headed for the café, singing under his breath, making a mental note that Bob's body seemed to have a tendency to low blood sugar; a meal and a night's rest had done amazing things for his outlook on life. And, since body and mind were—generally—linked, it hadn't hurt Sam's outlook either.

Rested, metabolism back in sync, he was feeling much more confident about being able to handle this Leap and make the necessary changes in history. All he had to do was convince Aline, and somehow he was sure he could.

Reentering the amusement park after visiting the café, he saw Mike and Jesse conferring over the partly disassembled corpse of the Spin-A-Whirl, a ride that suspended four passenger compartments from each of four main arms. The arms were supposed to rotate, while the suspended compartments spun independently at an angle of almost ninety degrees. Someone was experimenting with music over the loudspeakers, playing part of a tune and then stopping and starting over again. After the third time his humming along was interrupted, he gave up and went looking for Dusty to give him his marker.

Dusty was forking hay into the little corral under the intent supervision of Bessa, who was carrying a brown and white cat sagging over both arms, his tail dragging in the dust. The cat, nearly as big as the little girl, had blue eyes half-closed and a purr that Sam could hear from fifteen feet away.

"Good morning, Bessa. Who's your friend?"

The cat, still purring, raised his head sufficiently to indicate that a scratch between the ears would be acceptable. Realizing her burden was sliding from her arms to the ground like so much warm molasses, Bessa heaved him upward, trying to boost with her knee. The cat barely twitched. "This is Maxie," she informed Sam, puffing.

"Let me give you a hand there." He lifted the animal and settled it more securely in the little girl's arms. Maxie never stopped purring. "Looks like Maxie's a pretty tolerant cat," he observed.

The cat gave a desultory swipe to his hand with a rough pink tongue, as if accepting the compliment. Sam rubbed the velvety ears. "Hey, boy, nothing bothers you, does it? My old barn cats wouldn't let themselves be dragged around like this for a minute. I think I like you better."

Maxie gave him a cross-eyed look and put a kindly, possessive paw upon his hand. "Murrup," he agreed.

"Maxie's *my* cat," Bessa said, eyes narrowed.

"Oh, I'm sure Maxie knows that," he hastened to assure her. She snorted in a dignified fashion and slogged off, dragging the cat with her. The sound of the cat's purr trailed behind her.

Dusty, who had stopped forking hay to listen to the exchange, grinned and spat accurately in the opposite direction. "Jealous little soul, ain't she?"

Sam laughed. "I gave your receipts to Mizz Vera Schaeber," he told the other man. "Here's the marker. But there's something I want to take care of with Aline this morning. Do you mind?"

"Hell, no, boy, you do whatever you got a mind to. I can get these little dog snacks ready. *I* don't spook them." He considered briefly. "Not that I didn't appreciate your help yesterday, though. It's just that I didn't rightly *need* it, if you follow me."

"Oh, absolutely." Sam deftly shoved the troublemaking chestnut pony's quarters away from the fence and went looking for Aline Schaeber.

A large land turtle lumbered into the grass growing around the steps leading to the door of the office trailer. Inside, Mellie still snapped

150

her gum and examined her fingernails. Circles of sweat were already appearing in her armpits, and the fan on the file cabinet whirred busily without making an appreciable difference. Mike McFarland and Jesse, apparently finished with the Spin-A-Whirl, had their heads together over a roll of drawings, and Jesse was tracing something with a fingertip.

"Well hey there, if it isn't the master repairman! I see you got all the cotton candy out of your ears. How you doin', Bob?" McFarland was positively jovial this morning. "He tried fixing Miguel Castenada's spinner yesterday and damn near blew up the whole booth," he informed Jesse and the uninterested Mellie. "Lucky nobody got hurt."

"That so, Bob?" Jesse said. He had a look of I'm-really-going-to-hate-to-have-to-see-you-go, directed at McFarland, on his face.

"Not exactly," Sam said evenly. He still wasn't exactly sure *what* had happened the day before, and he didn't feel like discussing it with either of the other men.

"Well, no harm done," Mike said expansively. "We got it all cleaned up, didn't we, Bob?"

"We sure did." Sam made it a point not to emphasize the pronoun. Changing the subject, he went on, "Is Aline here?"

Reference to another female pulled Mellie's attention away from herself for a split second. "She never comes in to the office in the mornings," she mewed. "She's too good."

151

"That's enough, Melinda Mae," Jesse snapped. Mellie shrugged and returned to contemplating her fingernails. "No, Aline isn't here. Why do you want her?"

"I just want to talk to her about something," Sam said. He wasn't in the mood to improvise this morning. He wanted to accomplish his goal and move on, in every sense of the word. "Is she at home?"

"Probably."

"Courting the boss again, are you, boy?"

Sam stared at McFarland for a moment, feeling the muscles in his face harden. It was one thing when Dusty called him "boy." It was another thing entirely when the engineer did it. For a moment the scene blurred, so that he might have been back on Project Star Bright, when one of the supervisors had called him the Boy Genius and treated him like the new kid in town, trying to put him in his place. It hadn't worked then, either.

McFarland sensed that he had crossed some invisible line, and didn't quite know how to go about getting back on the other side without losing face. Before McFarland could begin to bluster, Sam nodded thanks to Jesse and turned on his heel to leave.

Unfortunately, he was turning to his right, and the weak leg gave a little. He caught and balanced himself on the doorjamb, waiting for the snickering behind him. It didn't come; the stumble wasn't obvious, then. But it did spoil a good exit.

But even that couldn't dampen his confidence for long. It lacked an hour to the park's opening time, and the jugglers were practicing in the Midway; the calliope was being tuned, someone was tightening down the last bolt to put a carousel horse, brave in gold and sky-blue paint, back on its circular path. The park must employ more than a hundred people, he thought, either directly or on contract, from the ticket sellers to the sweepers to the ride operators; it covered at least twelve acres, not counting the trailer space for the employees like Bob who lived more or less on the premises, and the parking lot for visitors. Then there were the food vendors, the security folks, the safety people. It was quite a busy enterprise, was Schaeber's, even before opening time, without visitors. Not that there were so many visitors after opening time.

It must take a lot of money to pay everybody, he mused. The insurance must be steep, too. No wonder Aline Schaeber was looking for a new attraction. The park had to earn enough money during the summer season to support most of these people through the winter as well.

It placed the high cost of admission in a new perspective. Maybe fifty cents wasn't too much after all, even in 1957. As long as the park was exciting, it was worth the cost. But if it had the same attractions it had had fifteen years ago, it was time for something new.

Al had said the accident was deliberate—it had been murder. There wasn't time, in two and a half days, to try to determine who had a motive to kill which victim, especially when he wasn't even sure who all the victims were yet. But if he could delay the grand opening even one day, that should change history just enough so that the "accident" could be prevented.

And he could Leap away.

CHAPTER
ELEVEN

This time he made it past the kitchen and into the front parlor. He had come around to the back to begin with, and Aline had greeted him at the door. She seemed to be glad to see him, and welcomed him inside without question, leading him immediately to the room in the front of the house.

The parlor window, draped in intricate, heavy knotted-lace curtains, looked over the front porch and lawn. The same lace was draped over the backs and arms of the overstuffed chairs as antimacassars. The room smelled faintly of lemon oil and disuse, everything dusted, everything perfect, a *House Beautiful* kind of room from 1957 or perhaps 1857, if one didn't look too closely. It was a very Victorian kind of parlor; the little tables beside the chairs were crammed with pictures of people, adults standing stiffly staring into the camera, children dressed in sailor suits and pinafores, eyes full of tears from being made to pose and hold still for the camera so long. The walls too were covered with pictures, group photographs and single shots, graduation pictures and picnics. He recognized one of Aline in a mortarboard from the store of high school yearbooks, and, shockingly, one of Bob Watkins, too.

But the vast majority of the pictures were of jugglers, clowns, rides from the amusement park. There was one of Dusty from years ago, holding the reins of one of his ponies, with a little boy wearing a cowboy hat and a grim expression, holding onto the saddle horn for dear life. There was another picture of Bob Watkins, a sheepish grin on his face, standing beside Jesse and a much older man who must have been Karl Schaeber, next to the sign by the amusement park entrance.

It made him wonder just what the relationship was supposed to be between Bob Watkins and Aline Schaeber, and he looked at her in a new light. She was the same age, according to Al, and the class pictures showed they had started school together. The brush with polio, though not as debilitating as the disease could easily have been, evidently had caused Bob to lose a year. Aline had forged on, and a gap was created between them.

Other people in Jasmine, knowing them both, didn't perceive it in the same way; Vera accepted him, if not as an equal at least as decent company. Dusty took it for granted that he was on a first-name basis with her. But when Aline invited him in, she took him to the front parlor to talk instead of the more informal kitchen. There were unwritten rules about meeting young ladies in parlors. Perhaps Bob had once had an expectation that the two of them would be closer than Aline wanted them to be? She seemed to want to maintain a distance between them.

She was attractive, of course. She had dark hair and violet eyes and a neat slim figure, and Al would probably be crooning to himself—where was Al, anyway? It wasn't like him to stay away this long. She was graceful and serious and intelligent and intent.

And while Sam found himself liking her, and understanding immediately why Bob kept pictures and dreams tucked away in a drawer, he found that he himself, Sam Beckett, wasn't particularly attracted. Perhaps he was looking for someone with a little less seriousness and a little more sense of fun. He wondered suddenly if she had many friends in Jasmine; it must be lonely for a single woman in her mid-twenties, trying to run a business in a part of the country that prided itself on its conservativism and old-fashioned values even in conservative times. Sam had to admire her courage as well as her looks, but he wished she would smile a little more. Aline Schaeber clearly had a heavy sense of responsibility and wasn't afraid of challenging the mores of her times.

Which, of course, complicated his immediate task more than just a little.

She was watching him as if he were preparing to pronounce the fate of the Western Hemisphere, not as if he were a friend or someone to be considered as a potential mate. Did Bob drop out of the running when he got sick? Would all this be easier if Bob were really courting her?

He could practically hear Al suggesting that he sweep the woman off her feet and talk her into postponing the opening that way. He smiled at the thought. Aside from the fact that he considered the use of such tactics dirty pool, it wouldn't be practical for Bob Watkins anyway. Bob could use his arm and leg, but they weren't quite strong enough for serious sweeping unless the lady in question was fully cooperative, and he didn't think this lady would take kindly to an abrupt approach of that nature. Few women did, notwithstanding Al's dreams of conquest.

"Is something funny, Bob?" She had a nice voice, too, pitched low and quiet. He hadn't had the chance to appreciate it before, what with the collapse of the booth and everything else going on. Her eye was better, too, he was glad to see. Maybe she was just under a little less stress in her own home.

It had been Bob's home too for two years, he reminded himself.

"No," he said hastily. "Not funny, exactly, I was just thinking about something somebody said. One of those things that was funny at the time, but . . ." He trailed off, unable to explain.

"I see." She folded her hands in her lap and waited expectantly.

He had the feeling that it wouldn't be good manners to broach the subject of the roller coaster immediately. One built up slowly to the topic of discussion, he recalled. Rushing into business all at once was for brash Easterners.

"I brought Dusty's receipts over yesterday," he offered.

"Yes. Vera told me about that. She did give you the marker for them, didn't she?"

"She sure did. Ummm—" *Oh, hell, I never was any good at small talk*, he thought, and plunged ahead. "Look, Aline, I wanted to talk to you about the roller coaster—"

She brightened immediately. "Yes, it's going to be wonderful, isn't it? I've been getting all kinds of calls. People are really looking forward to the opening."

"That's what I wanted to talk to you about. Are you sure about this?"

"What do you mean? Of course I'm sure. Don't be silly." She was genuinely startled at the suggestion.

"I mean, is it really safe?"

159

She opened her mouth to respond, then shut it again and studied him curiously, as if he were something strange and exotic under glass. "Have you been getting visions again, Bob? Is that what this is all about?"

"Visions?" The word caught him off guard. "Visions? I don't get visions."

"Come on now. You and I grew up together, remember? I remember what it was like before you got sick. And ever since then you've been seeing things and hearing things. And—" she faltered at the painful reminder—"after you moved in with us you used to tell us all kinds of things. So don't you fib to me now. Did you see something that bothered you?"

Evidently she believed that the sickness had resulted in brain damage and hallucinations. Sam supposed that was marginally better than being considered psychic. It was the pitying tone, the same tone he had heard her use when he first Leaped into Bob Watkins, that bothered him.

"I'm not a half-wit," he said, more sharply than he intended. "What if I did see something or hear something? Haven't I been right sometimes?"

He hoped he had, anyway. People tended to remember the few, coincidentally correct predictions and forget the thousands of wrong ones. Bob must have hit the bull's-eye at least once.

And evidently he had, because she hesitated. "Well, what *did* you see?"

"There's going to be an accident, and people are going to die if you open the roller coaster on Sunday. You have to stop it. You can't have the opening."

The words brought her to her feet as if pulled by an invisible cord. "Bob Watkins, that is a terrible thing to say, and it isn't true! It can't be true! You take that back this instant, do you hear me?"

Sam was on his feet too, trying to face her down. "It is true. The roller coaster isn't safe."

"No! I won't believe it! You must be out of your mind!"

A ripple of cold crawled down his spine. Fear made him say, "I am *not* crazy. Don't even hint it.

"That roller coaster isn't safe—look, all you have to do is move the opening. Check it out, get it certified by somebody—"

"On *your* say-so?" She laughed, without amusement. "Your visions?"

"Would it be so terrible just to check and be sure?" His voice sounded plaintive, even to himself, and for a moment he wished he could have the moment back to say it again in a different, perhaps a more emphatic way. Aline didn't seem to care.

"I've got all the advertising already distributed. People all over the state know about this. What am I going to say Sunday, oops, sorry, Bob saw pretty pictures in his head so come back tomorrow? Or next week, or next year, or

161

whenever you feel happy about it? We've already postponed things once. I can't afford not to open it Sunday.

"And besides, I *have* an expert working on it. Mike McFarland has worked on some of the biggest roller coasters in the country. He's already checked and rechecked, down to the last bolt and screw."

"Just one more time?" he pleaded, aware that he had completely lost control of the situation.

"If you're so scared of it, you don't have to come along for the ride."

He sat down again, shocked. "Was—was *I* supposed to be on the opening ride?"

"Of course you were, I told you months ago. Bob, how can you forget things like that? I swear, I think you're getting worse and worse as time goes on. I'm worried about you, I really am." Her eyebrows were knit as she studied him, as if looking for obscure symptoms.

If Bob Watkins had been on the roller coaster, was he—would he have been—one of the victims? A chill shot through him.

"Don't worry about me! What if something does go wrong? It's going to be a disaster, for you, for the park, for everybody. If people get hurt on that ride you're never going to recover from it!" *Especially if you're dead*, he added mentally, but was unable to say it. She was angry enough as it was. To suggest that she would be a victim of her own dream would be the last straw.

162

"Nobody is going to get hurt! Have you been talking to Jesse? Is this all his idea? Did he set you up to talk to me like this? Bob, I'm ashamed of you! You know Jesse is trying to—"

"Jesse has nothing to do with it! I'm just trying to warn you, it's going to happen!"

"Warn me? Or threaten me?" Her hands, held stiffly at her sides, were clenching and unclenching. "I know what this is. This is just your try to make me fail, isn't it? Just like Jesse's been saying, that I'm not smart enough to handle Uncle Karl's business. That I'm going to kill his dream and my dream both.

"Well, if I lose this opportunity it'll just prove you right, won't it? But I'm telling you right now, Bob Watkins, I've got too much money wrapped up in this, too many people are depending on it, and it's going to open on schedule. And neither you nor Jesse nor anybody else is going to stop it!"

There was a silence then, as she tried to find something more to say and Sam tried to find some way to respond. There was no way, and his shoulders sagged as he admitted it.

"Okay. Okay," he said at last. "I'm not trying to hurt you, Aline, honest I'm not. I wouldn't do that to you. I'm not that kind of man." *And neither is Bob Watkins.* "But please—please have it checked again. It can't hurt to have it checked again, can it? Just to be safe?"

She relaxed slowly, getting used to the idea that she'd won. After a moment she stepped

163

back, sat down again. As a truce offering, it wasn't a bad gesture.

"Of course it wouldn't hurt," she said graciously. "We've already got it scheduled, but I'll ask Mike to make it thorough. Every nut and bolt again, if you like.

"You could even help, if it will make you feel better. You work with Mike. I'll tell him you want to help."

Sam winced, envisioning how *that* bit of news would be received by the engineer.

Aline saw and understood. "I won't let him pick on you. I know you don't get along very well, but that's just his way. You have to be tolerant, you know."

And *that* comment was almost enough to make him laugh again.

"Tina, sweetheart—" he crooned into the telephone receiver. Al Calavicci's best friends, most of his random acquaintances, and all of his ex-wives would have recognized immediately the tone of his voice. He had messed up his personal life again, and he was trying desperately to recover the situation. It was happening with alarming regularity.

Al Calavicci was one of those men with the gift for regarding the current woman in his life as the only woman in his life, at least while the woman was in sight. His philosophy was one of serial monogamy, and his practice consisted of very short cycles.

Somehow, no matter how appreciative he was of a particular woman, no matter how intensely involved, something always went wrong, sooner rather than later. Usually the blowup was related to his appreciation of some other woman at the wrong time. He never meant to get distracted from the current love of his life; he was, simply, distractable.

The voice coming through the receiver was not impressed.

"Tina, darling, we need—I need you. I miss you. We *all* miss you."

The result was that all too often he was in the position of groveling over the telephone, trying to patch things up. His relationship with Tina had lasted longer than most, and this was the sixth or seventh time he had pulled out all the stops for a full apology, with roses and champagne. By any reasonable standard, both of them should have had the script memorized, and been able to cut to the happy conclusion.

This time, however, Tina had had enough. She had walked off the Project. And Al's voice was getting raw with desperation; this was not only his love life at stake, but his best friend's future as well. He had to get her back, for both their sakes.

Tina Martinez-O'Farrell may have looked like a classic airhead, who spent more time painting her fingernails than reading books and whose idea of intelligent conversation had to do with the best place to buy that darling little classic jacket, but classic airheads did not get top security clearances and access to classified projects. While it was true that Tina could price the casual observer's wardrobe to the nearest dime, she also held an earned doctorate in supercomputer architecture from Stanford. The reason her relationship with the Admiral had lasted as long as it had was that she was a sublime blend of brains and bimboness. The combination was one Al couldn't resist.

Unfortunately, it was also one that he couldn't handle. He kept focusing on the bimbo aspect of her perfect figure and gorgeous wide eyes and breathy voice, and losing track of the fact that she had the second highest IQ in the Project. Now he was trying his best to remember, by appealing to her sense of duty instead of playing to his hormones.

"Tina, honey, please, I know you're mad at me, you have every right to be, I was scum. I was worse than scum. I was—"

"You were *mean*." He could just see her lower lip thrust out, pouting, red, moist, quivering, inviting—

He cleared his throat, loosened his collar. "Yeah, you're right. I was mean. But Tina, please, listen, it doesn't matter if I was mean or not—"

"Yes it does!"

Closing his eyes, he rubbed at his forehead, wishing the headache would go away. When he spoke again, his tone was all business. "Okay. It matters.

"Tina, look, we have a problem here. Something's wonky with Ziggy, and we don't know how to fix it. The lights are going out. It's making funny noises. And it's telling us that it can't multiprocess anymore—"

"What do you mean, can't multiprocess? That's ridiculous. Multiprocessing is perfectly straightforward; it's all in the application protocols. There can't be any problem, unless you've been messing with the system cache." The words sounded wrong in that little-girl voice, too smooth to be a learned script and too light to be a mature woman.

"Oh, no," he assured her. "We wouldn't touch the system cache. Or the instruction processor either."

"Then I think you're making all this up." *So there*, came across the line.

"I wouldn't lie to you about this. I'm worried, Tina, really worried. Sam is caught in a real mess this time. I think whatever he's doing to try to fix things is going to end up trapping him there, and we can't get any information from the damned computer! Please, Tina, come back. Not for me, for Ziggy. For Sam." Al had never sounded so sincere in his life. He had never felt so sincere, either.

But Tina had heard a lot of sincerity in her time, and she wasn't buying it now. "Do you know where I am, Albert Calavicci? I'm sitting beside a pool in Palm Beach in my brand-new red bikini, and I'm getting a lovely tan, and I'm

167

drinking one of those drinks with a little blue umbrella in it. And there's this really gorgeous-looking guy in the pool and he's swimming back and forth and I think he's flirting with me. I think I'm going to let him buy me dinner tonight, and we'll go dancing, and *he* won't be thinking about some other woman and calling 'Beth, Beth!' in the middle of a *very* important moment."

There was a long silence.

"Al, are you there?"

"Tina . . ." Al whispered dryly, as much to himself as into the receiver. "You don't understand."

She heard, and her voice took on a distinct note of triumph. "You know what? I think that gorgeous guy is splashing water on me on purpose. And you know what else? It's really nice to be sitting by a *pool*, full of *water*, and surrounded by *palm trees*, instead of being buried in some old cave in the middle of nowhere, New Mexico. So I think I'll just stay a while and enjoy myself."

The sound of the disconnect and the dial tone beat into his ear, and he ground his forehead against the rough wall of his Spartan quarters and closed his eyes, his fingers clenched white with pressure around the handset. "Tina," he whispered. "Tina, Tina—"

CHAPTER
TWELVE

"If I can't get her to stop it, I'll have to stop it myself," he muttered. He paid no attention to the understanding smiles of the game operators, who twirled index fingers at their temples and shrugged to their customers. He was only crazy ol' Bob, after all, acting exactly the way everyone expected him to act.

Some of the maintenance people were cleaning up weeds that had grown up around the base supports for the Killer Diller. He stepped around them and moved to the operator's booth, looking it over.

The structure of the ride consisted of the uprights and beams to support the track along which the cars traveled, and the track itself. Running beside the track was a narrow maintenance walkboard, with a handrail beside the steep parts; the walkboard was solid until the track started to rise; then the beams became ladderlike steps and the handrail became a safety rope. Track, walkboard, rails and all made the structure about twenty-five feet wide at the lowest point, narrowing as it ascended.

In the middle of the track, bolted to the center beams, were the guide rails that the wheels of the cars followed when they swooped up and down and around. The ride had been built in sections, with a metal guide rail running down the center and retaining rails on each side. The cars would be held in place by all three.

The track was roughly oval, over a mile long, though the ride itself didn't take up nearly that much room because all the inclines and drops and loops squeezed it down. Parts of it dipped and twisted through tunnels. It could be clearly seen from the Midway of the park.

Sam crossed the tracks and the area within the structure to look at the tunnel. There was at least nine feet of clearance.

There, where that long stretch was by the operator's station, a set of air brakes was in place, ready to catch the cars and bring them to a complete stop at the end of the ride so the passengers could get out safely. And over here was the lever the operator used to open them. The friction surface operated like a clamp, two long slabs of steel, normally tight together, that would spring open and then shut again.

He walked along beside the rails, along the

wooden walkboard that ran next to the track, studying the chain that pulled the cars up the first steep slope to the top of the first drop. There was nothing else to move the cars along, and he realized that the whole ride, after the first pull to the top, was a matter of sheer gravitational force. The cars ran along the track in a controlled fall, building up energy as they spun around a coil and using it again as they climbed. The cars were kept on the guide rail by special wheels that kept them from flying off into space, or at least into the pond outside the fence.

Maybe something was wrong with the guide wheels that kept the cars on the rails. He looked at them closely and could see nothing wrong. But then, he probably wouldn't recognize a problem if he did see it, unless it was something egregious, like the wheels falling off or the rail hanging loose.

He poked at it. It remained stoically in place, with new bolts at the beginning and end of each section of track.

The frame of uprights and supports looked like a naked forest, or the cage of bars in the playground that they used to call a jungle gym. He could see where the walkboard changed from a solid path to a ladder as it climbed at a ridiculously steep angle.

"Gonna walk it with me?" came a voice behind him. "Gonna check it out?"

"I might, Mr. McFarland," he answered without turning around.

"I hear you're mighty concerned about this old girl," McFarland chuckled, slapping one of the supports in a familiar manner, as if the roller coaster were a milk cow he wanted to coax into moving over. "Hey, she's solid. I know that for a fact."

"Do you?" Sam murmured, still not turning around. He couldn't forget how McFarland had treated him—Bob—at the accident in the cotton candy booth.

McFarland, oblivious, was disposed to talk. "I sure do. I've walked every inch of this coaster. Designed it, helped build it. My personal achievement, you might say. You ever had something like that? Something you saw through from an idea all the way to the end?"

Sam filled his lungs, spreading his shoulders wide to get as much air as possible in his lungs, and let the breath go again, slowly, thinking about Star Bright and Quantum Leap. "Yeah, once or twice."

"Got to see things through. Make them your own. Got to put your stamp on something so they'll remember you when you're gone." From his tone of voice, it was important to McFarland that he be remembered. And it was clear that he was confident that he would be.

Sam turned around then, eyeing the other man's possessive grin. "Are you sure it's safe?"

McFarland looked amused and indignant at the same time. "It's what I made it. Going to

172

be the best known attraction in this part of the state. Maybe the whole state. People who ride Mike McFarland's Killer Diller are going to have the ride of a lifetime."

The Door opened somewhere behind Sam with a swoosh only he could hear, and a tension he wasn't aware of drained away. He was never aware of how much he missed Al until the other had been gone for a long time. And "a long time" could sometimes be measured in mere hours.

"That's for sure," Al said, commenting on McFarland's last remark. "Not that there's going to be too many of them. Or that they'll have too long a lifetime."

Sam was unable to face his friend directly while McFarland was around, but he could move, casually, so that he more or less faced them both. Al remained where he was. He looked very tired, more tired than Sam had ever seen him. His eyes were stark pits in his pale face. Even the insouciant green fedora, suspenders, and baggy pants only emphasized that the man inside was sagging from strain and fatigue.

"Is everything okay?" Sam couldn't prevent the anxiety from showing in his voice.

"Sure it's okay." McFarland thought the question was directed at him, and his response was a shade hostile. "It's going to do exactly what I want it to do."

"No, it isn't." Al, for his part, was ignoring Sam's question to continue commenting on McFarland. "We managed to get a little bit more information for you. Ziggy says the coaster still crashes—"

"I *know* that," Sam said impatiently. "I tried to—" Belatedly he recalled the audience. McFarland was watching him with a bemused expression. "I mean, I'm sure it's going to do what you want it to. It's just that I like to make sure of these things. I talked to Aline and she said I could go with you to check it out, on your last safety check, I mean."

"Oh, hell, *no*, Sam," Al said, jiggling the handlink. It shrieked in protest, and for a moment all but two of the lights blinked out. At the same time Al disappeared, at least stripes of him did; Sam shook his head hard at the sight of one-inch stripes of Al Calavicci alternating with one-inch stripes of roller coaster frame, trees, and landscape. Pieces of hand whacked at parts of handlink. With another mechanical scream, the lights fluttered back on, and Al was complete again.

The other man's eyes narrowed. "You want to look over my shoulder for the safety check? What's the matter, doesn't Miss Schaeber trust me? I've been doing this for twenty years!" When Sam didn't immediately answer, he snorted. "What's the matter with you? Got a mosquito in your ear? What are you shaking your head like that for?"

"Something I saw," he muttered. Al, unaware of the effect of the power dropout, continued to mutter, trying to read the tiny screen.

"Yeah, Jesse told me you see things. He says nobody believes you." The thought was giving McFarland pause.

"I guess it would be okay if you came along. You're pretty harmless, and if it keeps Miss Schaeber happy, well, keeping people happy is what the business is all about, isn't it?" He smiled. "Okay. How are you on heights?"

Sam looked up at the crown, seventy feet from the ground, and swallowed. "I'm okay with them."

"You better not be lying, boy. It's a long way down, and we're going to walk every inch of it. Tomorrow, nine o'clock. Got it?"

"*Sam*, I've *got* to talk to you!" Al was practically jumping up and down in his eagerness to get Sam's attention.

"Yeah, I got it." And then, to Al, "I've got it."

McFarland, satisfied, walked away whistling, his hands stuffed in his pockets.

Al started talking almost immediately. "Ziggy says that there's a ninety-eight percent chance that—"

"I know how to stop it, Al." Sam reached out to grasp the nearest upright, looking up at the forest of supports and rails and roller coaster track.

"Who's Al?" The voice behind him took him by surprise. He spun around, almost stumbling, to see Jesse waiting nearby. He must have been

175

standing there listening to the entire exchange between Sam and the engineer.

"Al, uh, well, nobody," Sam stammered, looking anywhere but at Jesse. "I was just talking to myself."

"Thanks a lot," Al remarked, without anger.

"So you're going on the final safety check." Jesse looked up at the frame too. "Aline asked *you* to go."

"Well, no." And then, in response to the arched brow, "She said I could go." It sounded lame, even to himself, especially in the face of the hurt in Jesse's face. "I'm sure she meant for you to check it over. She only told me because I'm so worried—"

"We don't need this damned thing!" he burst out. "It's too big, too complicated, too expensive! She knows that, and she doesn't want to hear me tell her. So she tells *you* to follow her fancy Shy-cago engineer around and make sure it's all right. Just like you know what you're looking at! You've never been good at fixing things in your life!"

"Jesse, I'm sorry."

It made no difference. Jesse didn't even hear him. "What's going to happen when the fancy Shy-cago engineer goes away? He's never been one place for a whole season in his life. I tell you this thing is going to be a trouble to us. Cost us thousands and thousands of dollars! And where we going to find that money? I tell Aline, and I tell ever'body, and nobody will listen.

"But they'll listen when he goes and *I'm* the one in charge—"

Jesse wasn't listening any more. Sam moved away, quietly, Al creeping beside him even though Jesse wouldn't have been able to see him if he'd been doing jumping jacks in his face.

Man and hologram left him behind as Sam headed back to Bob's trailer for lunch.

Al floated beside him, head down, passing through obstacles as if they weren't there— which they weren't, in the Imaging Chamber. Sam kept sneaking glances at him, trying to figure out what was wrong; Al avoided meeting his eyes.

By itself, this wasn't particularly unusual; Sam could think of any number of times when Al didn't want to look him in the eyes. Generally it meant Al had just done something that he knew Sam wouldn't approve of, and since there existed a whole catalog of things that Sam wouldn't approve of which Al did at any opportunity, a shifty gaze by itself meant little.

But he had never looked quite so exhausted and, yes, scared, before.

Sam had picked up a few things when he had gone out for breakfast. Once into the trailer, he dug out the peanut butter and began daubing it on a slice of bread. If Al, minutes before frantic to talk to him, now had nothing to say, so be it. Sam could wait. He had a Plan. He knew how to prevent the wreck.

"That's better with bananas," Al said.

Sam gave him a Look.

"Hey, if it was good enough for Elvis, why isn't it good enough for you?"

"Cholesterol," he mumbled around a mouthful of peanut butter.

"Don't give me that, *Doctor*. The cholesterol's in the peanut butter, not the banana. Even I know that much."

Sam took another huge bite. "Elvis fried his banana and peanut butter sandwiches."

"So put bananas on but don't fry them. You could use the potassium."

Sam swallowed, took a long drink of milk. "Speaking of potassium, what's wrong with you? You look like something the cat wouldn't drag in."

"Nothing." Al's lips tightened, and he poked at the handlink again. A light up in the right-hand corner blinked, and so did the fedora.

"Hey, what's wrong with that thing?" Sam put down the half-eaten slice of peanut-buttered bread and came closer to try to examine the instrument.

Al swung it out of his line of vision. "It's nothing. Nothing. We're working on it."

"Yeah? Who's we?" Sam asked, curious.

The shadow that crossed Al's face took Sam aback. "Hey, sorry, I didn't mean to ask. It's just that you have to have somebody working on those things, and—"

"You had somebody," Al said sharply. "Look, let's not talk about this, okay? It's getting fixed.

I want to talk to you about what Ziggy came up with on this Leap."

"So talk." There was more to it, he could tell, but Al wasn't going to give. He went back to his slice of peanut-buttered bread and took another bite out of it, washing it down with more milk. Every Leap had some simple pleasures. Almost every Leap, anyway.

"We got some more information," Al went on, still frowning at the link.

"So tell."

Al sighed. He was clearly more comfortable talking about this information than about the handlink. "Okay. There's a . . . ninety-eight point four percent chance that the person who sabotaged the coaster is one of three people. Ziggy narrowed it down to Jesse Bartlett, Mike McFarland, and—"

"Mike McFarland?" The idea startled him. He turned it over thoughtfully, considering, until Al interrupted his train of thought with the last possibility.

"Yeah." Al looked distinctly unhappy as he added, "Or Ziggy says it could be you."

Sam choked, almost spitting up his milk. "What? Me? I'm not going to cause any wreck."

"You," Al repeated firmly. "Not deliberately, of course not. But you might do something by accident."

Sam wiped up the minor mess and picked at a piece of peanut on the crust of the bread, not looking up. "By accident?"

179

"You're looking innocent, Sam." Al's voice was rich with distrust.

"You keep telling me I *am* innocent, Al." He smiled a cherub's smile, still not looking up.

"You're never innocent when you look innocent, no guy is. What were you going to do?"

"I still am," he announced, munching the peanut. There was a certain sadistic joy in teasing Al at moments like this. While Sam Beckett didn't actually possess a mean streak, he did have the gift of tantalizing his audience. It came in handy in writing project proposals, or driving his best friend crazy.

Al's patience was running thin, however, and he wasn't willing to play along. "You still are *what*?"

"I'm going to sabotage the roller coaster *before* the wreck. On purpose. So it's never going to happen."

Automatically, Al checked the handlink for the computer's latest update. While he knew intellectually that Sam's simple announcement shouldn't make a difference, it was still comforting to find out if the new information changed the odds.

It didn't.

He frowned as the readout remained obstinately the same. "Not according to this," he said slowly. "The odds aren't changing."

"Not possible." Sam swallowed the last gooey bite of peanut-buttered bread, working to get the remnants off his teeth. "If the thing can't start, it can't crash." It came out as an indistinct mumble, but Al understood him anyway.

"I can't help that. See for yourself. They're locked in. Nothing's different. Ninety-eight point four." He angled the machine so Sam could squint at the screen.

"No," he said, his confidence wavering only a little. "I know how to prevent it from happening. I saw it when I was looking at the framework—"

"Sam, if you know how to do it and you *do* it, then why haven't you Leaped?"

"Well, maybe I have to be here to do it. Maybe Bob wouldn't carry it through." He was rationalizing now, and both of them knew it. He turned away and began fussing with the milk carton.

"Or maybe your idea just isn't very good."

"Ziggy's been wrong before," Sam protested. "And you've been having trouble, you said so yourself. So maybe things are screwed up on your end."

He still had his back to the hologram, and didn't see Al wince. A thorough shaking didn't affect the readout either. "Nothing is screwed up on our end. We're just having a few minor technical problems."

Remembering the dropouts in Al's image, Sam laughed. "Then I think my odds are just as good as yours. I know what I have to do, Al. It'll be fine. Wait and see."

Two lights on the little machine blinked out,

and Al looked up and past Sam's head as if listening to somebody else. "Are you sure—"

"Yes," Sam said firmly, thinking that the hologram was talking to him. He realized his mistake when Al's attention shifted back. Al was not convinced.

"Look, I've got to take care of something. But I'm telling you, Sam, don't try whatever it is you have in mind. Either you don't succeed, or what you do actually causes the wreck to happen."

CHAPTER
THIRTEEN

"Gushie, did you find Tina?" Al was talking so fast when he left the Imaging Chamber that the programmer barely had a chance to get a word in edgewise. "Where is she? Is she coming back? What's gone wrong? What's happened?"

"If you'll allow me, Admiral," the voice from the air said. It sounded now like a woman in her eighties, quavering under a dowager's hump. "I've taken the liberty of speaking to Dr. Martinez-O'Farrell directly."

Al rotated in place, staring up at the high ceiling as if he could find the voice, or at least the speakers it came from. "And?"

"Please don't be so demanding, Admiral," the computer fretted. "I'm doing my best. It's my life too, you know. It's in my own best interest to bring her back as quickly as possible."

"Is she coming?"

"I believe I may have persuaded her." Even a quavering voice could sound smug.

"That's terrific!" The fatigue disappeared from Al's face as if by magic, and he grinned delightedly at Gushie. The programmer avoided his eyes. "Gushie, didn't you hear? She's coming back!"

Gushie remained silent, studying the thermal guidance indicators. Slowly, Al's euphoria drained away, to be replaced by suspicion.

"Tell me, Ziggy, just *how* did you persuade her?" he asked the ceiling again.

"I hardly think that data is germane to the issue," the computer responded. "The final outcome is what is important here, after all." The last few words were broken up, as if the voice record was scratched.

"Is that what Sam taught you, you overpriced hunk of scrap metal, that the ends justify the means?"

"No, Admiral. I learned that from observing you."

"What did you tell Tina to bring her back?" There was no lightness in Al's tone now. Hearing him, Gushie found something fascinating to do on the other side of the room. There were a lot of people occupying themselves with busywork to keep from talking to him today, one part of Al's mind observed. Another part waited, with growing dread, to hear just what kind of strings the computer had yanked.

"I explained that her difference of opinion with you was based on a misapprehension," the computer said. There was a certain hesitancy about it, as if it knew it was treading on sacred ground.

"And just what misapprehension was that?"

"I determined by reviewing the content of your last telephone conversation with her that she believed you were being unfaithful to her with a woman named Beth. She was, of course, mistaken; you are currently being unfaithful, as my dictionary defines it, with a woman named—"

"Never mind," Al growled. "That's Sam's dictionary anyway, and it needs updating. What did you say about—"

He couldn't bring himself to say the name. Ziggy waited for him to finish his sentence, humming to itself on a subliminal frequency as several centuries of computer time went by.

"Tina's coming back," he said, his voice dry. "That's what matters."

He left the control room without saying anything more.

Gushie looked after him, eyes moist. "That wasn't very nice, Ziggy," he whispered reproachfully.

"It was required," the computer answered.

Gushie, one of the few on the Project who knew the impact of what Ziggy had done, wrung his hands.

Once, years before, Al Calavicci had been married to a woman named Beth. But he was in the Navy, and on sea duty for months at a time; it had put the marriage under a terrible strain. But he had convinced himself that it was going to work out. And it might have, had he not been taken prisoner in Vietnam.

When he was finally repatriated, Beth, long since convinced her husband was dead, had married someone else. Al Calavicci had tried to change that particular piece of history in the course of Sam's Leaping, and he was unsuccessful; he had been given another chance to cut his own imprisonment short and had chosen not to. Since then he had rarely spoken her name. Not deliberately.

He sought Beth in his next four wives, in Tina, in innumerable encounters in which he never allowed himself to become close enough to a woman to threaten his idealized memories of his first marriage. He never told them about her. He never admitted his search to himself.

"I did what was necessary," the computer said, without mercy.

Judging from the hints and cues of the people around him, Bob Watkins was good at shilling the marks. At least that was what the barker in the next booth said, in between taunting and teasing passersby in to see the Bearded Lady (who took off the beard every night and went home to fix dinner for a pair of mischievous three-year-olds).

So he tried to lure them in. "Hit the ducks! Three tries for a quarter! Win big prizes! A stuffed animal for your sweetheart!"

Judging from the response, Bob Watkins had talents Sam would never share. "I'd be better off sticking to physics," he muttered to himself, as still another couple glanced at him and walked faster, tugging their children with them, to get away. The sound of Pat Boone and Elvis and Buddy Knox echoed from the loudspeakers.

He sat back on the stool and tossed a wooden ball from hand to hand. From where he sat, he couldn't see the roller coaster, but he could visualize it if he closed his eyes. All it would take was a stake jammed—*there*—and the ride would never start. No accident would happen. No one would be hurt. He could Leap.

Of course, that would just put him right back where he started, in someone else's trouble. Well, not exactly where he started—that would be too much to ask.

"Three shots for a quarter, get your ducks lined up and shoot 'em down, win a prize!" he yelled hoarsely.

He remembered a county fair one year when he and his brother Tom decided to win a prize from every booth and give them to Katie. He could still remember calculating the angle of diffraction necessary to make a basketball hit a board and land in an apple barrel that was shoved just a hair too far underneath. He'd made the shot, too.

He had been ten years old. Tom had tousled his hair. Katie had screamed with excitement.

187

For just a moment, the memory was so vivid that he almost expected to see Tom and himself wrestling with each other as they raced down the Midway, kicking up the dust, dodging in and out of the crowds. He could almost taste the sweet-potato pie his mother made every year, that every year took second place in the pie judging. Tom said it was because Mrs. Tomlinson, who won every year, was the judge's sister, but Mom always told them never to pick sour grapes, they were bad eating.

Sometimes the homesickness was almost too much.

"Three shots for a quarter! Knock 'em down! Step right up and fire away!"

The teenagers he was addressing gave him a wary look and detoured to the Frog Jump booth across the way.

"Hi," said a small voice. It was Bessa, with the ever-patient Maxie lying in the bed of a red wagon giving one satiny paw a thorough laving. "Where's the game people?"

"Hello yourself. I don't know. I guess they decided not to play today. Hello, Maxie."

The cat gave him an inscrutable, slightly cross-eyed glance and continued to work on the paw.

"Bob will be mad at you."

"Oh?" he said, hoisting her up on the counter, next to a stack of stuffed toys. "Why is that?"

"Don't know." The child turned shy suddenly, scuffing the toes of her Buster Browns together.

"Is it because I'm not doing his work very well?"

She nodded, her fine blonde hair flipping up and down.

"You'll have to tell him I'm sorry, when he comes back." Sam chirped to the cat, inviting the animal to jump up beside his mistress. For all the response he got, he might have been back in the future, as invisible to Maxie as Al was to adults in Jasmine.

"*You* tell him." Bessa didn't want to get into the middle of any apologies.

"I can't tell him, honey. When Bob comes back, I'll be gone. So you'll have to do it for me."

"No." She poked at a large pink stuffed chicken hanging from the inside wall of the booth, caught it when it swayed, stroking the soft plush. Catching Sam's eye, she quickly let it go again, folding her hands in her lap.

Sam sighed. Not even children cooperated with him. He wondered how he had ever managed to get a Project funded, much less built.

But the Project was far away, in time as well as space, and the most important thing at the moment, since he couldn't seem to attract any customers, was Bessa. At least she didn't have her finger in her mouth.

"Where's Al?" the little girl asked suddenly. "Al can tell him."

Sam thought about this. He could see himself trying to explain Project Quantum Leap, and Leaping, and Admiral Al Calavicci, and the artificial caves in the high New Mexico desert, and Ziggy, and time travel, to a five-year-old.

Bessa had her finger in her mouth again.

All right, a four-year-old.

"Yeah," he said. "We'll let Al explain it to Bob."

The park closed early on Friday nights; the Baptists, the Veterans of Foreign Wars, and the Elks all played Bingo, and there was a new movie on at the theater. Sam made one dollar and seventy-five cents at the duck shoot and awarded four stuffed toys as prizes. He had a feeling that the cost-benefit ratio was not working in his favor. At least he didn't have to worry about collecting tickets, the way the ride operators did.

Bessa had wandered away, dragging her red wagon, complete with cat, behind her. Sam wondered who and where her parents were. Everyone seemed to know her, and no one was concerned that she was by herself. Of course, it *was* 1957, and there weren't many crazies in small towns in Oklahoma, so she was probably okay.

Al still hadn't shown up. He wondered if there was more going on with Ziggy than Al had told him. Sometimes the time flow was in sync and sometimes it wasn't; he didn't know what the variables were anymore. It was possible that someday he would remember, out of the blue, the same way that he remembered the taste of sweet-potato pie and Katie's scream; it was possible that someday he would remember the "rules" of Leaping.

It was possible that someday he'd be President, too, but he wasn't betting on it. Right now he was going to concentrate on stopping that roller coaster. Somehow stopping the roller coaster would be the trigger that made him Leap. He didn't care about Ziggy's ninety-eight point four percent. Ziggy had been wrong before. He repeated it, like a mantra: "Ziggy has been wrong before."

He put the money in an envelope and got the tarpaulin from underneath the counter. It was awkward, tossing it over the top of the booth; he had to consciously remind himself to use both hands. Bob would probably have far more use of his right arm if he exercised it more often. As it was, the body he occupied resisted him, and it was frustrating. More often than not when he was Leaping, he could overcome those limitations that were more mental than physical, but bodies had habits just as minds did.

He paused to catch his breath. The temperature was in the nineties, and so was the humidity, and he decided to go back to his trailer and get a very long drink of water before anything else. Besides, it might give Al more of a chance to get back to him with the improved odds. And they'd be improved, he was sure of it. They had to.

As he passed a flowering bush something flickered at the periphery of his vision, and he jerked back, thinking he was being buzzed by a large bumblebee. The "bee" hovered, investigating a blossom. He held very still, watching, and was rewarded when the hummingbird lit for a moment on a branch and cocked its head at him inquiringly. It was less than half the size of his hand.

"Hummingbird, hummingbird, fly away home, your house is on fire, your children alone," he murmured. He held his breath, waiting for Al to pop in and tell him he had it wrong, it was "Ladybug, ladybug . . .", but nothing happened.

He got his drink and cleaned up the minor clutter in the trailer, still stalling, waiting for Al. He couldn't put his finger on why it bothered him so much that the other man wasn't there; perhaps the handlink's acting-up was making him nervous. Maybe he was too reliant on Al, getting to the point where he couldn't function any more without him. Maybe he needed to learn how to get along without him.

Maybe he'd *have* to learn to get along without him, if Ziggy broke down one day. If he got stuck in a Leap. In some other Leap.

"The hell with it," he said at last, and left the trailer, headed for the Killer Diller.

He saw Mike McFarland talking to Melinda as he passed the office. The teenager was fluttering her eyelashes and fluffing her hair, smiling her best sparkling smile at the sophisticated man from the big city, doubtless believing that he was smitten with her. The only other people left in the park were the people employed there, the vendors and maintenance and security people. He exchanged greetings with them, waves and smiles, and wondered who they were. They all knew Bob; Sam knew perhaps a dozen whose names he'd picked up in the last couple of days. He managed to avoid being pulled into conversations, invitations to dinner, and all the rest, and forged against the stream of people heading for the exit, heading for the coaster.

He had to linger, waiting for the last few to go away. He busied himself with checking out awnings and tiedowns, looking in on the ponies and feeding them scraps of alfalfa, hoping he gave the impression to anyone who might be watching that he had a legitimate reason to stick around. The sun was sinking by the time he was alone with the ride.

In this, at least, his memory did not betray him. He climbed up the passenger steps to the operator's station and studied it again, rehearsing what he intended to do. The wooden stake he had seen lying on the ground beside the first frame support had been moved, and for a panicky moment he thought he would have to find something else, but it was propped out of the way behind the sign announcing the Grand Opening. Balancing it like a javelin, he knelt beside the track and examined the chain in the center of the incline track.

The chain in the middle of the track was a foot wide, bordered by rachets to prevent the cars from rolling backward and the first guide rail to keep it in place. It extended from the operator's station to the crown of the first drop, where the cars would be released to the force of gravity. He regarded the pitch of the walkboard and the height of the crown and decided that he could just as well disable the mechanism from ground level.

All it would take was lifting the chain out of its track, or jamming it so that it couldn't move. If the chain couldn't move, the cars couldn't move either. Ergo, no wreck. It was simple, efficient, and practical. The only possible drawback was that the sabotage might be discovered too early, and fixed. He had to jam it inconspicuously, to delay the opening long enough that it would be postponed.

Presumably, postponing would be enough. Ziggy's history said that the accident happened on Sunday, July 14. If it was delayed, there would be time for McFarland to uncover the problem and solve it.

As usual, theory was simpler than practice. To begin with, the squared-off end of his stake didn't fit between the links of the chain. For another, an inconspicuous place to put it wasn't immediately apparent. He walked from one end of the operator's station to another, poking, wishing that Bob carried a pocket knife so that he could at least whittle the stake into a wedge. He walked past the four linked cars, with their fresh paint and green padded seats and safety bars, and red lighting stripes along the sides and the words "Killer Diller" in clean white italic letters.

He turned around and walked back down, past the cars again, and at the other end of the track he finally found the place he sought. The chain sagged just the smallest bit at the end, creating an opening.

But the stake still had a squared-off end, and it wouldn't fit. After four or five tries he tossed it away in frustration. The sun was setting, and the shadows of the frame and supports made a cage of the amusement park.

A frantic search of the area around the ride revealed nothing. McFarland must have made sure everything was put away; even the buckets and stray pieces of wood were gone. It was amazing enough that he'd even found the stake. He was getting desperate; he had to do this while there was still light enough to see what he was doing. There was a tool shed by the trailers where he could find wrenches, but if he went back there someone would see him, question him, stop him.

But Dusty had a pitchfork for mucking out the ponies' corral. He jogged, stumbling every few steps, over to the pony ride and found it, shoved into a bale of straw. It might yet be possible. He glanced at the setting sun. It would bring no relief from the heat, but at least the glare would be gone. He should still have light to do what he needed to do.

But there was still movement in the amusement park. He could hear voices, coming closer. He returned to the roller coaster in a clumsy half-run, falling to his knees on the passenger steps and hauling himself up again with the support of the handle.

Poking the tines at the chain, he saw with relief that they would slide in easily. The voices were louder.

He poised the pitchfork in place, placed one foot on the shoulder of the tines, and pushed. Behind him he could hear shouts of inquiry and alarm. He ignored them, leaning into the chain.

And continued to lean, toppling, as Jesse, coming from the side, tackled him, pushing him into the handrail.

Behind Jesse, Aline Schaeber stood, red-faced with fury. "Bob Watkins, have you gone completely crazy? What do you think you're doing?"

"And Ziggy has been right before, too," he muttered. So much for mantras.

CHAPTER
FOURTEEN

When he was five, his father had given him an empty can to play with. He could still remember the bright silver metal, how the points of the jagged edges had gleamed in the sun. It had been beautiful, that can.

Daddy had grinned at him. Paid attention to him.

He could still remember the cut across his hand. It didn't hurt at first. He couldn't remember it hurting later, but he knew that it didn't hurt at first, when the edges of his soft pale palm gaped open and the dark red blood welled up and dulled the shiny edges of his tin can.

He could still remember the sound of his father, laughing.

● ● ●

Tina got into the airport in Albuquerque very late. Al was there to meet her, pick up her luggage, escort her back up the escalator from Baggage Claim through the terminal to the small plane hangar. She sniffed when she saw him, but didn't say anything. He kept his peace as he loaded the King Aire, shoving six bags, two cosmetic cases, and three shoe boxes into the hold and bowing her into the copilot's seat.

Usually he enjoyed the opportunity to fly again, even if it was only a six-passenger jet. This time he performed the pre-flight check in grim silence. Tina leaned her head back, careful not to muss her glossy, high-piled red hair, and pursed her lips, making a show of staring out the windshield into the dark New Mexico sky. The lights blinking in her fashionable earrings were a counterpoint to the control panel. Engine noise provided an excellent excuse for the two not to talk during the trip.

In less than two hours they were landing on the stretch of road that served the Project as an airstrip. From the air, the Project looked like a cluster of weatherbeaten cinderblock buildings with tin roofs, an abandoned ranch where someone had forgotten to turn out the lights. Brown, withered tumbleweeds clustered against the windward side. There was nothing there to attract the eye, or the curious. They were met by an armed guard as Al folded down the three steps of the little jet. The guard checked their identification and faded back into the darkness.

"That's one of the things I hate," Tina said at last. "Those guards. Why do they always have to, like, carry guns and things?"

Al shook his head. Tina did have an irritating habit of commenting on the obvious, and he wasn't in the mood to cater to her.

"Well, aren't you even going to talk to me?" she went on. She made no move to help him carry the luggage to the van parked at the end of the airstrip. Al made several trips back and forth, feeling a great deal like Gunga Din.

She was wearing high-heeled sandals and a very tight skirt, totally unsuited to walking even a short distance in the desert. She wobbled as she went, and Al couldn't help watching any more than he could help breathing. He might be irritated at Tina, or more properly at Ziggy, but that had nothing to do with a certain visceral pleasure.

"Well, aren't you even going to say hello?" Tina said.

"Ziggy is breaking down," he said, starting the van, forcing himself back to business. Tina needed to be briefed on the technical situation in order to do her job; it didn't mean that Al had to engage in small talk.

He didn't feel like small talk. He was unaware of how unusual his behavior was. Tina was watching him out of the corner of her eye, as if waiting for some comment, some gesture, some reaction recognizably Al's.

When it did not come, she asked, "What do

you mean, breaking down? Do you mean, like, rusting? Or error messages? Or—"

"I'm not a computer jock," Al interrupted. "You'll have to talk to Gushie for the details. But the circuits and the microprocessors seem to be failing, and we don't know why. Ziggy isn't talking at all anymore. We can only communicate through the terminals. Gushie says it's a hardware problem."

"Gushie would," she sniffed. "He won't admit that programming might be the problem. Dr. Beckett approved it. He thinks that anything Dr. Beckett did has to be, like, perfect."

"I wouldn't know about that." Al wanted a cigar in the worst way. One of the first rules of the Project was a ban on smoking within the Project buildings; so many of them were underground, with a circulating air system, that a cigar savored in the living complex could be smelled almost anywhere in the complex. He had submitted with bad grace. There was a whole catalog of rules and regulations about the complex, mostly due to the fact that when you took Government funding, you also took Government auditors busy looking after their Government funding, and Government rules and regulations for them to audit your compliance with, along with the account books. The fact that the Project was in the middle of practically exactly nowhere turned out, in this case, to be a blessing.

Unfortunately, as far as the no-smoking rule

went, the Project Director considered it an unbreakable health and environmental consideration. So even if the auditors did a desk audit from Washington and never set foot among the cactus and scorpions—site reports always emphasized the cactus and scorpions—he still couldn't smoke in his own quarters. Al had always wondered sourly if Sam would be quite so adamant about it if he had a tobacco habit of his own. It wasn't as if Al smoked cigarettes, after all.

They stepped through the ramshackle-looking solid steel door into another world, clean and carpeted and colorful. The upper room was a recreation room, with a grand piano in the corner, and a small kitchen. Tables were stacked against one wall. On those rare occasions when most of the people on site were free, they could be set up for a party. Otherwise, meals were strictly on your own. The other ground-level buildings held administrative offices and one or two other buildings, mostly for camouflage.

The rest of the Project was underground, in the caves and tunnels. Al escorted Tina to the elevator, hauled in the luggage, and slumped against the side until it came to a stop at the residence level.

"I really, really hate these teensy rooms," Tina said. "They look just like *dorm* rooms, you know?"

Actually, Tina's looked more like a dorm room in which a Laura Ashley catalog had exploded.

She was the only woman in the Project who had a king-size bed, gracefully draped with a lacy canopy and matching dust ruffle. The table next to the bed was also draped in lace. The camelback sofa was covered in a tapestry pattern. She had even created a window treatment over a poster of the beach at Waikiki.

Al, who had seen it all before, dropped the luggage in a heap and went back for more, leaving Tina to turn in place and exclaim over the room exactly as if she had never been there in her life. By the third trip he had it all in, and Tina was waiting for him.

"What the *hell*?"

She was dressed in the filmiest of negligees. As he dumped the last of the shoe boxes she extended her arms to him. He started to step forward, glands on autopilot, and jerked himself to a stop. "What are you doing?"

"Well, Al, I thought you'd want to welcome me home. . . ."

"Tina, honey, I'd love to welcome you home—Lord, I would love to. . . . But we don't have time. We've got a problem here." He edged away from her as she advanced on him, licking suddenly dry lips. "Tina, please, don't do this to me. I'm serious, we're in trouble here."

"Oh, Al, I know about Beth," she cooed. "Ziggy told me all about her, I *understand*, honey. Come here."

It was like a dowsing with ice water. Suddenly Al was an Admiral again, facing a crisis, emo-

tions shut down. Even Tina could see the trans-
formation, and her arms dropped as she stared at
him in confusion.

"Get some clothes on, Tina," he snapped. "We
need you in the Control Room. Or haven't you
been listening?"

"Well, of course," she sputtered. "But I
thought it could at least wait until morning.
It's late."

"Pretend you're still on California time." He
turned on his heel. As the door slid open, he
added without turning around, "By the way,
don't ever mention Beth to me again, Tina. It
isn't appropriate."

"Bob Watkins, what on earth has possessed
you?" Aline was furious. "What are you trying to do, spoil everything? Why? What did you
think you were doing?"

Jesse looked up from examining the chain.
"No damage done. Caught it in time. Doesn't
even need fixin'." He stood up and brushed his
hands together. "Looks like Bob here has gone
right over the edge."

Sam could see the conviction hovering behind
Jesse's faded blue eyes. *Lock him up, he's not
safe. Sees things, talks to himself, now look
what he's doing. Lock him up. Put him away.*

"No," he burst out. "You don't understand.
I don't want to hurt anybody. I don't want the
ride to hurt anybody! Please, you have to listen
to me. . . ." He lunged, caught at Aline's arm.

203

She pulled away, but he hung on.

"You get your hands off her," Jesse snarled.

Aline stopped struggling, and Sam let her go, letting his eyes talk for him. She seemed held by them for a moment, and then shook free. "Bob, I know you wouldn't hurt anybody, not on purpose," she said firmly. "But don't you see, you could have caused an accident to happen, disabling the chain."

Jesse's attention was diverted briefly to the woman, apparently surprised that she had recognized what "Bob" was trying to do. Sam took a deep breath. Aline was not stupid, not incompetent, and not about to pretend she was in order to build up the egos of the men around her. It would be a good attitude to have in the near future; it meant things were tough for her in the fifties. Jesse's reaction was proof enough of that. He looked outraged at her knowledge.

"It wouldn't have caused an accident," Sam said. "It would have prevented one. The coaster is going to crash on Sunday, and seven people are going to die unless you put off the opening."

The two of them stared at him, openmouthed, and for a moment he cursed his own impulsiveness. And his focus on Aline had prevented him from seeing Jesse's split-second reaction to his words, so he still didn't know if the man had guilty knowledge or not.

"Bob Watkins, I do believe you really are going crazy," Aline said at last.

"Oh, boy," he whispered.

"I'll talk to Judge Grant," Jesse said with grim satisfaction. "He'll take care of this. We'll get a commitment order."

"No! No, don't. You don't have to do that. I didn't really cause any harm, did I? You don't need to do that. Aline, come on, you know me. Don't you?" He was scared, and he didn't care if they knew it. They couldn't possibly know just how frightened he was at the prospect of being put away.

"Bob, you're talking like a crazy man," she said gently. "We can't have you going around saying such awful things. People might believe you. You work here, after all. They'll think that you know something bad about the ride, and they won't come."

But I do know something, he almost said. *They've got to believe. They've got to stay away.*

But if he said it, she would nod resignedly to Jesse, and they would come after him with a piece of paper and lock him away.

She was waiting. Jesse was waiting.

Sam was shaking.

CHAPTER

FIFTEEN

Tina was dressed in her lab clothes, a white one-piece that fitted her like a second skin. She was tracing circuits with one elegant, painted fingernail.

"So, like, where is everybody?" she said, oblivious to the dozen or so other people at work deep in the guts of Ziggy.

"Almost everybody was on leave when this happened," Al said. "We only called back the ones who were technically necessary." He handed her another page of diagrams, liberally stamped SECRET in large red letters, top and bottom. The lower right-hand corner contained a box with the drawing issue codes. "Have you found anything yet?"

"Well, give me a chance, all right? I told Dr.

Beckett when he put this out here that the power was dirty. You must have a couple of hundred surges and dropouts an hour in this musty old place."

The desert was not a place that Al would have described as musty, exactly, but as long as Tina was in the proper mood, he wasn't going to argue semantics.

"There looks like an itty-bitty problem here," she said to herself. "Now some of this stuff you really need Dr. Beckett for. It's *his* design, you know, not mine."

"If there was any way we could get him here to work on it, we would," Al said through his teeth.

Tina didn't notice his tone. "Like, for instance, right here, this is real interesting. I don't think I've seen this before. It isn't in the design."

"What do you mean, it isn't in the design? That's the most recent issue, isn't it?" He raised his voice. "Gushie? Isn't this the most recent drawing?"

Gushie sidled over, rubbing his hands together. "Well, it's the most recent I could find. There might be another one in Dr. Beckett's office, but that was the one in the files." He smiled apologetically at Al. "I don't have a key to Dr. Beckett's office."

No one had a key to Sam's office any more, except Al. When Sam had stepped into the Accelerator and for all intents and purposes vanished, Al had quietly taken all the keys and kept them himself. It wasn't exactly a shrine, and he would have hotly contested any such accusation, but he didn't want anything changed for the time when Sam came back. He always claimed it was hard enough to find things as it was.

"Well, I can't work with something this far out of date. Look, it isn't the same at all." She shoved the paper into Al's hand. "What about the program? Is there something in the program that requires this kind of stuff in here?"

"There do seem to be some new things," Gushie admitted, "but I thought they were just things I'd forgotten about."

"And you didn't tell me?" Al was stunned. "How could you not tell me?"

"Sir, I wasn't sure. Besides, I didn't think I could explain it to you. It's a programming thing."

"Yeah, right," Al said savagely. "And I'm just a deskbound former jet jock, right?"

Gushie winced.

"Okay." Al was seething as he threw the drawing onto the floor and marched out again, leaving the other two staring after him, appalled.

Sam's office was on the other side of the Waiting Room, and Al paused to look in. For a change, there was no one in the observation deck. All the monitors were throbbing peacefully, the lights all the proper colors, with needles tracing brain wave patterns on graph paper. The body on the bed looked rested, relaxed. Even the right hand, lying across the chest, was limp, rising and falling with the steady working of the lungs.

It looked like Sam. It was a nearly perfect image of Sam. It was the same height, same face, same dark hair with a single wisp of white at the left temple. The hands were the same elegant, musician's hands. Someone who had only known Sam Beckett from pictures would have identified the body on the hospital bed immediately, without question.

They would have been wrong.

The body on the bed opened its eyes, and the mind that looked out was the mind of Bob Watkins, polio survivor, high school graduate, carny operator at an amusement park in Jasmine, Oklahoma, sometime psychic, terrified.

In the observation deck, green monitor lights blinked red.

The man on the bed gabbled, and strings of saliva dripped down his chin. Al flinched. From the box on the stand, he pulled a tissue and dabbed the mouth dry as if the patient were a baby.

The brown eyes rolled up, and Sam Beckett's body went limp again.

Al closed his eyes, crumpling the tissue in his fist, and turned away.

Al had only been in Sam's office a few times in the years since Sam's first Leap. At first, when he was trying to accept the idea that maybe Sam would not be coming back immediately, he used to come in and sit quietly in Sam's chair, swiveling back and forth on the cracked brown leather, looking around at the clutter of books and papers and disks and notes, reading over the collection of classic Far Side cartoons stuck on every available surface. There was a collection of Beckett family pictures on the wall, Sam's parents and brother and sister; other pictures, like the one of his high school orchestra's state competition prize trip to Carnegie Hall, the one of him accepting his first doctoral hood.

His gaze skipped over the deep-dented easy chair where he used to sit late into the night, trading insults and ideas with his best friend. It was easier than sitting in his old chair and seeing Sam's empty one. He could remember all too vividly a conversation he had had with Sam in this very office, before Ziggy was up and running, while they were still trying to figure out how to use the tissue circuits. Sam, staring at the pictures on the wall.

"Did you ever have something you wish was different, Al?" he had asked idly. "Like if you had done something different, your whole life would have changed?"

"Sure, every time I proposed." Al had waved his unlit cigar in an expressive circle. "I can think of quite a few times my life would have been different."

"Yet if you changed it, you wouldn't be the same person now." He was looking at the picture of his family, of his brother in green fatigues, his eyes narrowed and thoughtful. His brother was laughing into the camera lens, his arm flung

around the shoulders of one of his buddies. In the background was jungle, and a river. The picture had been taken by a famous war photographer the day before Tom was killed. It was one of Sam's most precious possessions.

"Sure. I'd be a lot richer. Save myself a fortune in alimony." Al propped his feet up on the desk, too, carefully avoiding a thick volume of microcode, and sipped at a glassful of pale golden liquid that wasn't supposed to be (since it was after all a government-funded project), but was, Chivas Regal. They'd made a breakthrough, and they were celebrating. Down the hall, they could still hear the cheering of the rest of the Quantum Leap team, echoing oddly down the cave tunnels. Tomorrow they would be back at it, wrestling with how to create the proper Instruction Processor for a new kind of computer, but tonight they could let off some steam.

"Like Tom," Sam said, sliding down in his chair and leaning back to study the acoustical tile in the ceiling.

Al winced, looking at the level of his friend's glass, which was considerably lower than his own. Sam was not normally maudlin. He didn't sound maudlin now, just—thoughtful.

"If Tom hadn't died in Vietnam, I couldn't have stayed in school. The farm—well, you remember what it was like, back in the seventies. Farms were failing, MIT was expensive, even with a scholarship. But Tom died, and

212

he'd made me his beneficiary so I could stay in school." Sam took a deep draft of his drink. "I wouldn't be here today—none of this would be here today—if Tom hadn't died." He finished the drink, picked up the bottle, swished the remaining liquid around a time or two, and put it down again without refilling the glass.

"But you know, Al, I'd give it all up in a second if he could walk through that door."

"You don't know that you wouldn't be here," Al argued. "You'd have found a way to stay in school. You couldn't not go to school. Not with your brains."

And Sam had smiled and shrugged that self-deprecating shrug. "Maybe."

"No maybe about it," Al said loyally. He had finished his drink and refilled it.

"And there's other things," Sam went on, not bothering to address Al's protestation. "I wish I could change other things—"

He never finished that sentence, though. Never spelled out what the other things were he wanted to change. Never said whether they were deep in the past, or closer to the present.

"Time," Sam murmured. "Changing time. It would be like solving a crossword puzzle in four dimensions, making sure you don't change the wrong things. Like cat's cradle." He chuckled. "String theory.

"You'd have to preserve randomness. You'd have to make sure you didn't try to change things deliberately, make them what you think *they are. You could really screw things up that way—"*

And he was gazing into space again, running a mental program of his own.

And the result was that Al never knew if he managed to do it, if he managed to change the things he really wanted to in his own life, or in others'.

There was something, though—maybe it was Tom's dying, maybe it was something else—that drove Sam to create a way to look at the past, had driven him from the very beginning. When the multi-tetraflop computer alone couldn't do it, with billions upon billions of calculations a second, he had decided that what a computer needed was not just fuzzy logic but the power of human inspiration. He had gone after and gotten a doctorate in medicine so that he could better understand the human brain, in physics and electrical engineering and other things so that he could design the tissue cells for the new computer, named Ziggy in a moment of desperate facetiousness. He had found a way—Al did not want to know how, but he always wondered if that lock of white hair was connected to it somehow—to use his own brain cells.

And when, after Ziggy was up and running, the cells of Sam Beckett alone were not enough, he had conned, begged, inveigled his best friend, Al Calavicci, into donating some as well. It had been the most terrifying thing Al had ever done, submitting to that biopsy, even though it hadn't actually involved bits of his brain; for some reason clear only to Sam, only a sampling of nerve cells was required. Still, the government hadn't known; their Ethics in Human Experimentation committee would have had kitten fits. Al didn't know the source of Sam's passionate intensity. But it had been that melding of nerve tissue that permitted Ziggy to link Sam to Al, now, so that Al could appear to Sam as the "hologram."

An empty whisky bottle, filmed with dust, sat on the floor next to the brown leather chair. Al shuddered and shifted his gaze away.

Tina had observed once that Sam's handwriting had the tall loops of ambition and the sharp points of intelligence; he could see it in the notes on the desk pad, equations, circuit sketches and diagrams of human brain cells, notes scribbled in German and French and Japanese, telephone numbers and cost calculations.

Al's eyes narrowed. Last time he had come in here, trying to feel in touch with his friend again, he had idly scribbled a note of his own beneath a minor equation, where Sam had balanced his checkbook. This time the note was scribbled beneath the title of a German journal article.

He wondered which one of the changes Sam was making in history had resulted in this tiny change in the present, and how long he would remember the difference. No one else ever seemed to notice.

Perhaps it didn't matter. Perhaps, as he had

215

said to Sam that evening in his alcoholic haze, the things that were supposed to happen would happen anyway, no matter what Sam did. Even though every time Sam made a change it changed the input to Ziggy enough that whole sections of history had to be reprogrammed, causing the computer to "lose" its creator in history for varying periods of time. Ziggy tried to predict the changes that would make it most likely that Sam would be able to Leap back into his own body in the present, but something or some*one* else kept getting in the way. So things changed unpredictably. Again because of the link through Ziggy, Al could remember how things used to be, though there had been so many changes it was beginning to be difficult to keep the ever-shifting pasts straight.

And it was almost as lonely for him, Al, being the only one who remembered everything, as it was for Sam, who could remember hardly anything at all. And there was no point in telling Sam about things that his very Leaping was in the process of changing. That would just screw Ziggy up that much more.

And perhaps one day Sam would make such a difference that whole people, or the whole Project, would wink out of existence. He wondered if he would remember that when it happened, or where they would all go. Worse—what if only Sam was gone, replaced by someone else? Or if he, Al Calavicci, never met Sam Beckett at Project Star Bright, never became the Quantum Leap Project Observer, never donated those cells?

There were times when he was just as well pleased he confined himself to the practical side of physics, he thought, unconsciously rubbing an unobtrusive scar on the tip of one finger. Transdimensional temporal theory made his head ache. Al Calavicci preferred to live in one present at a time whenever possible.

The present he lived in now, for example, had no picture of Tom on the wall at all.

He stood, searching for the rolls of drawings that might be undocumented changes to the Project computer. They could have been anywhere, tucked behind the computer terminal, stuffed into the bookshelves along with textbooks and fiction and models of the human brain. Sam had wanted his computer to be as much like the human brain as possible, only more so. Al used to think he had succeeded too well. Now he was sure; it looked like the computer was subject to human ills as well.

He went through everything, checking each drawer, each shelf. He found nothing. He tried again, looking everywhere, even underneath the chairs.

That was the trouble with instability. There might have been drawings, sometime in the past, sometime in some past. But there were no drawings now, and no way to know if there ever had been. He could come back and look again tomorrow, hoping that something in the past had caused drawings to appear where today there were none, but that didn't make sense. If the computer had changed because of new drawings, the drawings would co-exist with the changes. If there was any sense to causality, Ziggy's hiccups had nothing to do with changed plans.

He threw up his hands in disgust, flinging papers. Maybe Ziggy was changing itself. And in that case they were in real trouble.

When he was twelve, his best friend's father caught his hand in a table saw. He could remember the bright arching spray of blood, so pretty in the sunshine. And the piercing scream, once the shock had passed and the man had realized his hand was gone.

He could remember the screams, the metallic smells of blood and machinery all mixed up, the look on his best friend's face when the boy had seen his father's hand cross-sectioned and the three fingers and part of the palm on the other side of the saw. The pretty pattern of droplets that the sawteeth flung into the air.

The excitement. His friend's mother coming out from the house, concerned, and the change of expression on her face when she saw her husband on his knees in the sodden sawdust, clutching at his wrist in an effort to stop the pulsing flow. People running back and forth. Ambulances. Sirens. Noise. Tears. Shouting. Being jostled back, so he wouldn't have such a good view.

And milk and cookies in the kitchen as neighbors got them out of the way, talking about the terrible accident in low voices, glancing at him and his friend with worry, with compassion, with concern, with more cookies in their hands.

It was wonderful.

And all it had taken was removing one vital screw so the safety lock would fall away . . .

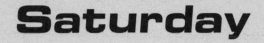

Saturday

CHAPTER SIXTEEN

Sam Beckett stared up into the darkness, sweating in the humid night, grinding his teeth. Somewhere, unheard, a clock chimed midnight.

He was naked, unable to stand the touch of clothing. He could feel straitjackets and air movement through jeans sliced for electrode contacts, the edges of manacles biting into his wrists, the cold gluc of the paste to transmit electricity against his temples. Silent, he could not stop screaming inside.

Leaps were blurring. The asylum. Death Row. Therapy. Electricity. He remembered now. Electroshock . . . Madness . . .

The shadows of the window blinds fell like bars against the wall. Behind the throbbing of the ceiling fan he could hear voices, dozens of voices, all of them his voice.

Outside, crickets chirped high and fast.

The muscles of his throat were locked open. The air stank of panic, sweat, and jasmine.

If he renounced the warning, the truth, he would be safe. Safe from the straitjackets and the electrodes and the bars and being trapped forever and ever in a place where there was no way out, where they poked and prodded him and examined him like a laboratory rat and eventually, eventually they would strap him in a chair and put a hood over his face and he would die. . . .

His fists clenched, and he keened without sound, caught in unwanted memories, physical and emotional. There were two Leaps, his rational mind knew, maybe more. There had been one where they killed him, not him, the man into whose life he had Leaped, he *hadn't died*, Jesus Ortega had died. And another one, the one he shut his eyes against and thrashed his head back and forth against the flat feather pillow, the one with beatings and shock and loss of everything.

Sweat rolled down his ribs. He dragged his breath in, forced his eyes open, stared up into the lazily turning vanes. He was Sam Beckett, physicist, caught in one of his own experiments like a rat in a maze, and the only way out was to follow the path, whatever it was, to the end.

Sometimes rats found dead ends. That was all right. Real science located the dead ends too.

In this particular maze, the cheese at the end was Leaping again, out of here, away from the threat of the asylum. To Leap, he had to prevent the wreck.

His panting began to slow as he clung to the chain of logic like a lifeline. He had faith, when he was sitting in the electric chair in Jesus Ortega's body, waiting for 10,000 volts, that he would Leap in time. He could have faith now too.

He couldn't prevent anything if he were locked away for observation. He couldn't accomplish anything from a mental ward. Therefore, logically, he mustn't do anything that would put him there. And if that meant looking Aline in the eyes and saying, "No, I was wrong, there won't be any wreck, nothing's going to happen," then that was the correct thing to do.

So he did the right thing that afternoon, backing down from Jesse and Aline. It only felt like sheer gutless shameful cowardice, folding to the threat of being put away. It only felt like a betrayal of the truth. It was really the proper scientific thing to do.

He couldn't help it if the alternative gave him nightmares.

His shuddering quieted. His hands relaxed.

He knew what Al would have told him. Sometimes you do things you don't want to do, because you have to. He could recognize the necessity. He could accept it without embracing it. The thing that troubled him still—the muscles in his neck were softening—was that he had so cravenly accepted the easy way out.

But it was done, like it or not, and now he was back where he started.

Outside his window, a cat wailed like a child in anguish. Maxie, he thought, on the warpath, transformed from the languid little-girl's-pet to essential animal by the light of the full moon.

He listened as the cat met a rival, or a mate, and the wail rose to a shriek. Someone in a trailer not far away yelled and threw something, and the yowling stopped short. Even the crickets were silent; the only sound came from the rotation of the ceiling fan and his own breathing.

He had to find another way to stop things. He needed more information; where was Ziggy? Where was Al?

How had the odds changed?

The fan continued to spin, hypnotically.

"Sam! I'm glad I caught you." Al was looking a little better, but the white suit and matching Panama hat still made him look washed out.

"Where have you been?" Sam challenged, rinsing off his breakfast dishes. "What's going on, anyway?"

"We've been taking care of things," Al responded. "It's okay now."

"Oh, really?" Sam arched one eyebrow in exaggerated fashion at the handlink, which was still obstinately dark in one corner. "It doesn't look like it."

"Hey, we're doing the best we can." Al was doing his injured act.

Sam shrugged, conveying clearly that he was not inclined to buy it, but wanted to get on with things.

"Besides," the hologram went on shrewdly, "you don't look like you had such a hot night yourself. What happened yesterday?"

"That doesn't matter now. Al, what does Ziggy say?"

Al could tell when Sam was avoiding the question. "It's still at ninety-eight percent. Are you sure you're all right?"

But the other man was obstinate. "Ninety-eight even? The odds have gone down?"

"If you want to call that down, I guess they have. But now Ziggy says the saboteur's either Bartlett or McFarland. We still can't tell which." If Sam didn't want to talk, he wouldn't talk, and wild horses couldn't make him. Al dropped the subject.

"We already knew that." Sam stacked the dishes in the drainer. "It never was me."

"It never was Bob," Al corrected, as if it didn't matter. "Now we know he didn't do it, even by accident."

Sam flinched. Al pretended that he didn't see that either.

"Do we know how it happens?" Sam was putting things into the icebox, his back to the other man's image.

"Something about the rails, and a brake fail-

227

ure. Apparently it was hard to tell from the evidence—afterward." The readout blinked, and he muttered under his breath, "Tina, dammit—"

"What did you say?"

"Nothing. Nothing. We're just getting the last little glitches smoothed out, that's all." He muttered to himself and to Tina and to whatever gods might be listening as the readout jittered again.

"Well, I'm certainly glad to hear it," Sam said dryly. "Got any bright ideas? The opening is tomorrow. We're running out of time."

Al shook his head. "If we knew which one it was, we could try to stop him. Ziggy says there's at least a sixty-six percent chance that whatever it was that caused the accident was done just before it happened. I guess you could try to pin down one or the other of them."

"I'll start with McFarland," Sam said instantly. "You go see what you can find out about Jesse Bartlett."

"Huh? That doesn't make sense. McFarland's the stranger here. I could probably pick up more about him, doing research about where he came from before he got to Jasmine, while you could—"

"No." Sam stopped himself an inch from slamming a glass into the countertop, lowered it very gently the last half-inch so that it met the linoleum with the smallest of clicks. "You go find out about Jesse. I don't want to deal with him."

"How come?" It was an expression of honest surprise, followed rapidly by suspicion. "What *did* happen yesterday?"

"Nothing that made any difference. Look, just do it, okay? If you find out something, center on me and let me know. I'll be asking around, seeing if I can find out anything." He sucked in a deep breath, staring up at the ceiling. "Al—"

"Yeah?" Al responded, when Sam didn't go on. "What?"

"Do you have any new information on what happens to Bob?"

Al looked away. "That doesn't seem to have changed."

"I was afraid of that. . . ."

Mellie was in the office, snapping her gum, trying out a new nail polish. It was too pink for her complexion, and it clashed with the new henna red of her hair. The office reeked with the scent of her floral perfume, a cheap drugstore brand, but Sam was more interested in her mind than in her fashion sense. He knocked on the jamb of the door.

Unfortunately or otherwise, Bob didn't meet Mellie's criteria for being either a customer or rich, powerful, and/or handsome, and so wasn't considered worthy of her attention.

Still, it was worth a try. "Hi" he said, in his best seductive fashion.

"I told you last week I wasn't going to go out with you, Bobby James Watkins," she said, not looking up from her nails. The brush slid across the cuticle of her little finger, and she tsked in irritation. "Now look what you've made me go and do!"

Clearly Bobby James Watkins was no more the Lothario than Sam Beckett was. Sam gave it up and tried for the direct approach. "Mellie, what do you know about Mike McFarland?"

Mellie blew a large pink bubble. "I know he's just about the most beautiful man I've seen around here in a long time," she said. "And he's sophisticated. Not like *some* people." The sideways glance of the copper-brown eyes made it clear to whom she was referring.

"How long has he been here?"

"You know that as well as I do," she sniffed.

"Well," he improvised desperately, "I don't know how long it took him to notice you. How long has he been paying attention?"

He figured, with some justification, that Mellie would assume the man had noticed her as soon as he set foot in Jasmine. It wouldn't occur to the girl that a stranger might not notice her, be attracted to her, fall head over heels in love with her.

A strange, "echo" memory of Bob's reminded him of a time when someone had pulled out a chair for Mellie at a church social, and someone else had talked to her, indulging some innocent middle-aged lust. She had come away convinced that all those married men were in love with her.

He blinked, shaking his head. He wasn't supposed to be remembering Bob's memories. Maybe this was one of his own, some woman in his own past too much like this young girl in front of him.

"Well, just as soon as he walked in the door he came over and said hello," she said smugly. "He's been trying to get me to go out with him for three months now."

Three months? That was longer than Sam had thought. Still, if McFarland was involved in building the roller coaster, it made sense. A thing that size didn't go up overnight.

"Why'd they pick him, anyway?" he said, picking idly at the leaves of a rhododendron wilting in the corner. "What makes him such a hotshot?"

"Why, Robert James Watkins, are you jealous?" Mellie's eyes sparked. "I thought you were just sweet on Aline Schaeber all this time."

"Well, what do *you* think?" It was always safest to turn the question around, Al had told him once, late at night over a bottle of beer. Ask a woman what she thought, and nine times out of ten, she'd tell you. At length. In detail. With subreferences. Then you didn't have to think of anything to say; she'd do all the talking for you. Sam had considered the attitude a little narrow-minded at the time, but acknowledged that with some women, there was some truth to it.

And Mellie, of course, obliged, thereby proving once again that even clichés were true sometimes.

Opening her eyes wide, she tossed back her hair, flirting for all she was worth. Bob didn't have to be rich, famous, or handsome; all he had to be was the only male present. He was good enough to practice on. "Well, I always thought you were just the sweetest thing, just miles smarter than anybody else around—"

"Including Mike McFarland?"

"He's just visiting."

"So he's going to go back to Chicago soon?"

"Well, he only came to help out with the roller coaster. Isn't that the most exciting thing? I can't wait to ride it. But I might be scared. It *is* so *tall*. Would you ride it with me?" she asked artlessly.

It wasn't bad, he had to admit. If he really were Bob Watkins, he'd have just been maneuvered into escorting Mellie Mae on the Killer Diller. And no doubt afterward buy her some cotton candy, and win her a toy, and take her home. All part of 1950s courting ritual. He could see the road to the altar reflected in her shining eyes, and he backpedaled, fast.

"I don't think I'm going to be riding it," he said. "I don't know enough about the man who built it."

"He's done lots of roller coasters!" Mellie said indignantly. "Just hundreds!"

"Oh, come on, nobody's built hundreds of roller coasters."

"He did so, he listed them on his résumé. Here, I'll show you." She got up, shaking her hands energetically to dry the nail polish, and marched over to the file cabinet. It took a certain amount of maneuvering to open the cabinet without spoiling the still-wet polish, using the pads of her fingers and the palms of her hands. Finally she got it open, and paged through the contents with her knuckles.

"Well, you might *help*," she said, noticing him still standing on the other side of the room.

"Oh, yeah, of course." But she didn't move away, and he ended up standing rather closer to her than he meant to. Her arm brushed against his chest as she pointed to the file, and she gave him what was supposed to be a blinding smile.

"It's that one."

"Right." He grabbed it fast and stepped away, and she looked confused and more than a little hurt.

But he was busy paging through the slim sheaf of papers, absorbing information as fast as his eyes could skim over it.

Mike McFarland might not have "hundreds" of roller coasters to his credit, but he did have at least a dozen. He had moved around a lot in the past twenty years. And, interestingly enough, each time he had gone to a smaller and smaller place, working his way down the civic ladder, until now he was in Jasmine, Oklahoma. The letters of recommendation were glowing enough, but guarded too, as if the writers weren't quite sure what to say about the man.

Perhaps he had a drinking problem, or chased women, or something of that nature. There seemed to be no question of his technical competence. And he seemed to be liked. It wasn't as if the people who wrote the letters had to make the man sound good to get him off their hands; he was employed for short periods of time, to design, build, and train operators for roller coasters, and at the end he would move on. There was nothing in the file to tell why he had fastened on roller coasters for a living. Sam wondered if there was a whole tribe of people out there, some specializing in Ferris wheels, some in carousels, some in Tilt-a-Whirls, moving from amusement park to amusement park in pursuit of a vagabond living.

"You better give me that back," Mellie said nervously, as he stopped to scan a newspaper article about the opening of one ride in St. Louis, Missouri. "I don't think you're supposed to see that."

"Probably not," Sam agreed. He had finished almost everything anyway, and he could call it up for mental review later—one of the advantages of having a photographic memory. Even if the photograph sometimes developed unexpected holes. He handed the file back to her, just as Aline came into the office, carrying a stack of colored paper.

Mellie scurried back to her desk, shoving the incriminating file underneath herself and sitting on it. Aline, looking at "Bob," didn't notice.

"Bob, how are you doing this morning?" Her voice was tinged with wariness.

"I'm just fine, thanks." He wished he could figure out why he didn't find her particularly attractive. She was looking remarkably fresh considering the morning heat. Her plaid shirtdress looked as if it had been freshly pressed, and her carefully applied makeup was without a flaw. Beside her, the younger girl looked even more garish.

She moved well, too, and her voice was pleasant to listen to. With a start, Sam realized that perhaps he wasn't quite as indifferent to the park owner as he thought he was.

"Hey, she's pretty." Sam jumped. It was Al, of course, and the two women looked at him with narrowed eyes.

"Is something wrong, Bob?" Aline asked delicately.

"No, nothing. Nothing. Just got a little chill, that's all."

"Somebody walked on your grave," Mellie said knowingly.

"Now *she* looks like a party waiting to happen," Al observed.

"You just looked like you—saw something." Aline was waiting for him to deny it again. Sam swallowed.

"Hey, she's observant, too." The holographic observer seemed far happier than he had been in recent days.

Sam bit back the impulse to comment, and

chose his words carefully. "Appearances can be deceiving."

"I suppose so," Aline said doubtfully. "Well, I'm glad I saw you, anyway. These are the final flyers for the opening. Can I trust you to put them up for me?" She held them out to him, her hand shaking just the least bit.

"You know you can trust me," Sam said before he could stop himself. Aline's reaction, pursed lips and a shifting of the eyes, was less than he could have wished for. She, too, remembered the confrontation yesterday. The only blessing was that she seemed unwilling to repeat it. Mellie looked back and forth between the two, totally confused.

"Well, I'd like to think I can," Aline responded. "I'd appreciate it if you'd put those up around town.

"And Mellie—" she handed the girl a handwritten note. Mellie had to lean to get it without letting the file she was sitting on slide to the floor. "This is the final list of the people who will be on the ride for the opening. I'd like you to get it typed, and then do those invitations the way we talked about it. The Mayor and I will be in the front car, and Mrs. Jenkins and Mr. McFarland in the second one, and Sheriff Kennally and his little boy in the third. We'll put Mr. Davis from the Elks Lodge and Tessie Rodriquez in the last one. Hop to it, now. Those have to be delivered this afternoon."

Sam saw his opportunity. "I'm going to go

now. Thanks for the advice, Mellie, I'll be sure to—to soak my hands like you said. Goodbye—"
He couldn't help but think of it as making an escape, scooting out of the office without waiting for formal farewells, flyers clutched in his hand. More than anything he wanted to be away from Aline's searching eyes. He didn't want to be around when Mellie finally stood up, either.

"What did you have to leave for?" Al complained. "I wanted to look some more."

"And I don't want to give them any more ammunition to think I'm nuts, if you don't mind."

"Then you better quit talking to me in public. People are watching."

Under his breath, Sam said a word he didn't normally use, and headed for the only quiet place he could think of at this time of day, the trailers. Al floated alongside, still talking.

"I had Ziggy do a search on Jesse Bartlett. He found a lot of stuff on the Bartlett family—I guess they used to be pretty big shots in this part of the state, back before the Crash. But it turned out they didn't have any oil on their farm—well, they did have three wells, but two were dry and the third one just gave out. And they had a family gift for bad business decisions. Sold IBM stock and bought automatic basketweavers. That kind of thing."

Sam went up the steps and into the trailer, and Al floated through the wall beside him.

"Okay, you're safe now, so talk to me. What

did *you* find out?" Al tried to lean casually against the counter, and miscalculated a fraction, so that he appeared to be leaning *into* the counter instead. As Sam grimaced, he glanced down and realized what he was doing. "Rats, I can never get this right."

Sam expelled a long breath, couldn't prevent himself from glancing around to make sure there were no witnesses to see him "talking to himself."

"McFarland seems to be on the level. He's got experience in building the things."

Al nodded. "That's what I thought. I think Jesse's it, Sam. It was common knowledge that he resented Uncle Karl's takeover. And he's got the knowledge, he's been working on the rides for years. Motive and means, Sam."

"And opportunity—nobody'd question him." Sam closed his eyes, concentrating. "Something else, too. Is Ziggy okay? Does he have a fix—"

"Not yet. But we're getting there, we're definitely getting there. What were you going to say?" While Al didn't want to talk about Ziggy, at least he was back to his old jaunty self.

He must have made up with Tina, Sam thought, smiling to himself. He smiled again at the feeling of wry pleasure that brought him. Still, it didn't have anything to do with the problem at hand.

"It can't be McFarland," he said. "Didn't you hear Aline give Mellie that list? Mike McFarland is going to be riding that roller coaster, in the second car with the banker's wife. That means he must have been one of the victims. If the wreck was deliberate, he'd never have made himself a passenger."

"You're right. Now the problem is—what do we do about Jesse?"

CHAPTER
SEVENTEEN

Tina Martinez-O'Farrell sang softly to herself as she studied the wiring diagrams. Since Tina couldn't carry a tune in both hands, it was fortunate that Gushie, standing next to her, was tone-deaf.

"What do you think's the matter?" Gushie had a habit of showing all his teeth when he was nervous. He was very nervous standing next to Tina.

"I don't know." She stuck her lower lip out, a gesture that Gushie found profoundly moving. "I don't understand what's going on. Let me see those orders again."

Gushie handed her a sheaf of papers, sweat-stained where he had been clinging to them for the last twenty minutes, and she smiled understandingly at him. He shuffled and wrung his hands and grinned some more.

"These are orders for repairs and new peripherals. Who signed these?" Sometimes, the airhead image that followed her around, a miasma of silly, superficial concern, was more transparent than at other times. Tina looked like the kind of woman who could have slept her way to a doctorate—at least, enough professors had hinted as much—but she found her subject so, like, interesting, she didn't notice she was being hit on. Shortly after she successfully defended her thesis, her committee chairman took to drowning his lost opportunities.

"I, uh, I didn't look?" Gushie was asking as much as answering. He resembled nothing so much as an old illustration of Tweedledee from *Alice in Wonderland*: prism-shaped, with a wide mouth and large, moist eyes magnified by thick glasses. He wore trousers held up by wide suspenders and said things like "Contrariwise" to foster the impression. "Uh, that one, it looks like the Admiral signed that one."

"And it looks like *you* signed these two."

Startled, Gushie stopped sweating long enough to snatch the two orders in question out of her manicured hand. "I never did!" he protested.

"And this is *my* signature!" She looked up at the frame of the computer, indignant. "Ziggy, I know I never signed these. I wasn't even here that day. I was in Santa Fe, and I have the shoes to prove it."

Ziggy did not respond.

Gushie gasped, holding out still another order with a trembling hand. "Look!"

Tina took it, spread it out against the side of the computer rack. "Beckett?" she read wonderingly. "Dr. Beckett signed this? He couldn't have. He hasn't been here in, like, years and years. And this is dated two weeks ago."

"Maybe he came back," Gushie said, nervously looking over his shoulder as if the Project Director was going to step out of the Accelerator to confront them at any moment.

"No, he didn't," she said positively. "Al would have told me if he came back, even for a minute."

"Then how—"

"Ziggy, you've been a bad computer," Tina said sternly, her hands on her hips. "Shame on you, forging signatures! What were you trying to do? Al is going to be really mad when he sees these."

Gushie was bewildered. "Ziggy is forging signatures? How can it do that? Why would it do that? I don't understand. . . ."

"Ziggy is a very smart computer, y'know," Tina explained kindly, giving the mass of metal and plastic a fond, exasperated glance. "I guess he wants to get even smarter."

"But that isn't in the program," the chief programmer protested. "I know it isn't. I didn't put anything like that in there."

"No," Tina said, patting the cabinet as if it were the cheek of a loved nephew. "You didn't

243

have to. You put in that fuzzy-logic stuff Dr. Beckett was so excited about, and I guess it just fuzzed and fizzed until Ziggy started programming himself."

"Are you nuts?" Gushie burst out. "That's not possible. That would mean Ziggy has volition."

"That's right," Tina agreed, rolling up the drawings. "You gave him an ego—"

"*I* didn't do that. That was Dr. Beckett's idea. You can't say *I* did that—"

"Okay, okay, so Dr. Beckett gave him an ego. I think losing Dr. Beckett hurt Ziggy's pride, so he decided to, like, rebuild himself so he could do a better job finding him." She looked sternly at the cabinet, which held rack upon rack of components. "You didn't have to do that, Ziggy. You could have come to me. Now look at you. You made yourself sick."

"You're talking to it as if it really does understand," Gushie said nervously.

"Well of course Ziggy understands. But he's not very experienced. He's overbuilt himself, and we have to put him on a little diet, that's all."

"Ziggy on a diet?" Gushie looked ill. "Overbuilt himself?"

"That's right. But we've got it all under control now. We'll just trim off some of these extra circuits."

"But where," Gushie inquired desperately, "did they *come* from?"

Tina regarded him pityingly. "From Zigs. He just made up the orders and forged our names to them. The technicians thought they were just doing regular maintenance and repairs. They didn't know they were actually changing the architecture."

"You're saying this computer has volition," Gushie whispered. He peered around at the cabinets surrounding them, their working lights reflecting in the sweat filming his brow. "Like Colossus."

"You've got to stop reading that science fiction stuff," Tina chided him. "It's all weird and people won't like to talk to you."

"What will Ziggy say if you—change it back?"

Tina paused, screwdriver in hand. "Oh. I didn't think of that." She nibbled her lower lip in a fashion that would have sent Al Calavicci, if he had been there to see it, into palpitations. "I think I'll wait to reconnect his voice until *after* we fix him," she said brightly. "Who knows, maybe it'll go up an octave."

Breaking and entering had never been one of Sam's strong points. The look he shot around himself as he tried Jesse Bartlett's back door would have tagged him as a burglar in the mind of the most casual observer. Al stood beside him, tapping his foot on empty air; since Sam was standing on steps, Al had to hover to remain at eye level. Sam tried not to look down.

"Well, are you going to go in or not?" Al said. "The door isn't locked."

"Brilliant observation," Al snapped. "The better for you to enter with. Will you get in there? Somebody's going to see you."

"I don't feel right about this," Sam said.

"I'm not surprised." Exasperated, Al floated through the wall and began nagging from inside the house. "Come on already. There's nobody here but just us holograms."

"Right," Sam sighed, and pushed the door open. Before Al could start in on him again he stepped inside and closed it behind himself. "Al? Where are you—*don't* do that to me!" Al was floating in the ceiling, checking out the upstairs without bothering to locate himself entirely on location, as it were. Sam snatched futilely at the dangling feet, his hand passing completely through the holographic image. "Will you come *down*!"

"About time you got here." With a tap on the handlink and an obedient beep, Al was standing next to him. Sam glared. Imperturbable, Al began poking around the kitchen in which they were standing.

"This is not right," Sam muttered. There was nothing in the kitchen that looked like evidence—not that he would have recognized evidence if he saw it, since he wasn't sure what he was looking for evidence of. What would constitute evidence of a planned multiple murder?

Besides, it felt like an invasion of privacy. Sam left the kitchen and went into the dining room. It was very much like the dining room in

Aline Schaeber's house, with its dark heavy furniture and wide-planked wooden floors, but it was smaller, and the curtains were fraying at the edges, and the windowsills were covered with a layer of dust. The glass in the china cabinet was filmed and hard to see through. A blue and white china tureen held pride of place on the sideboard, but the ladle was chipped. Clearly, Jesse Bartlett lived alone.

There was nothing here, either. Sam went into the next room, the front parlor, with Al trailing after, commenting on the arsenic-green wallpaper.

The sofa was covered with plastic. The brown leather of the old club chair in the corner was cracked and worn. This was a front parlor which hadn't seen guests in quite a while; a filing cabinet and a table in the corner testified that it now saw duty as an office. Sam glanced out the windows at the street, wondering if someone walking by could see the stranger going through Bartlett's papers.

"You didn't tell me Aline Schaeber was so pretty," Al said, as Sam pulled open the first drawer.

Sam stopped in the act of pulling out a file, glaring at him. "Am I supposed to take notes on every female I see and report to you?"

"Well, sure," the other man responded, surprised. "You're supposed to notice things like that. I mean, even *you* have to notice things like that."

"I'd ask what that crack is supposed to mean, but I should know by now," Sam muttered, paging through the file. There was nothing remotely incriminating in it, and he stuck it back and pulled another. "Could you just once keep your mind on your business?"

"I do, all the time," leered Al. The expression vanished as he caught sight of a roll of papers stuck between the file cabinet and the wall. "Hey, Sam, look at this. This could be something."

Sam replaced the file he was looking at and unwedged the roll, a set of drawings rolled into a cylinder three feet long and bound with a rubber band. Al craned his neck to see over Sam's shoulder as he stripped off the rubber band and carried the roll into the dining room and looked around for something to hold down one end.

The soup tureen did the job nicely. Placing it on one corner and the ladle on the other, Sam spread the paper out.

"Hoo, boy," Al said. "You still wanted evidence? I guess this is it."

"Not necessarily." But the protest was feeble, and both of them knew it. What they were looking at was the main construction drawing for the Killer Diller. It showed the climbs and drops and loops and twists, the scaffolding of the support system. The drawings beneath detailed the motor underneath the operator's station which would operate the chain, pulling the cars up the first drop, and the brakes set at various locations to slow the ride down at strategic points.

And all over the drawings were markings in thick black ink, in what had to be Jesse Bartlett's handwriting, with notations about height and speed and angle, with comments and exclamation points. Jesse had studied every aspect of the ride, identified every weakness. There was even a calculation in the corner of one page about how many passengers it would take to earn back the cost of building and operating the ride, with the contemptuous, "Impossible!" scrawled beside it. One corner of Sam's mind observed, in incidental fashion, that Jesse had failed to add the numbers correctly.

"That's it, then," Al said. "It's definitely Jesse. You've got to stop him."

"Yeah, but *how*? I've tried talking Aline out of having the opening, I've tried wrecking it myself—"

"So that's what you were doing. . . . I take it that didn't work either."

"No. It didn't." He rolled the papers back up and slid the rubber band over them again, worrying a folded corner free, replacing them carefully behind the cabinet as if they had never been moved. Every movement declared that he didn't want to discuss the attempt further.

Al watched, head tilted, savoring the moment. After a brief internal struggle he decided to forego the pleasure of saying "I told you so" and find something more constructive to offer.

"You could always try talking to Jesse yourself," he said. "Maybe if he knows that some-body else knows, he won't do it. Maybe that will be enough to stop things. At least for the time being."

"If he just delays it, that means somebody will die later on."

"But you'll have Leaped."

Sam closed his eyes and took a deep breath. "But people will still die. If I'm supposed to prevent that—"

"Sam, people die eventually anyway. All you're supposed to do is give them a little extra time, not make them immortal. Nobody's immortal."

"No," Sam agreed sadly, "I suppose not." The faces of his brother and father flashed before his eyes, together with a sense of confusion. Were they dead? He thought so, but— He couldn't recall. He started to ask his companion, and stopped himself. Some things he didn't want to know.

Al, who knew Sam well enough to know the question and also knew too many versions of the answer, stepped up the pressure. "Look, go find Jesse. Talk to the guy, at least. The opening is tomorrow. You haven't got much time. Ziggy says whatever was done to the ride was probably done tonight."

"Okay. All right. All right!"

Soon, soon, it was going to be soon, all the glorious screaming. They would fly through the air like so many rag dolls, they would squish when they hit the ground like water balloons dropped from a great height, such a great height.

And they wouldn't know it was him, no they wouldn't, but he would know, and he would have his revenge. They would respect him. The ones who lived would respect him.

They'd have to. Or accidents would happen to them, too.

CHAPTER
EIGHTEEN

The sky was darkening as he made his way from Jesse Bartlett's house back to the amusement park. Wind whipped the trees, tearing away the green leaves. As he entered the park gate he could see a brown and white cat that had to be Maxie trotting purposefully along ahead of him, ears back and tail straight out, looking for shelter. He hoped that Bessa was with her parents, whoever they were.

There were even fewer people than usual at Schaeber's, and the patrons there were casting anxious glances at the sky. Sam paused, and Al shook his head. "No such luck, Sam. There's a thunderstorm tonight, but tomorrow's going to be bright and clear. Ziggy says the opening still goes on as scheduled."

He couldn't find Jesse. Mellie, flirting with McFarland in the office, didn't know where he was. Miguel at the candy stand hadn't seen him; Dusty, untacking his storm-spooked ponies, shook his head and spat a negative stream of tobacco juice. The maintenance people didn't know, the ticket takers didn't know, the ride operators didn't know, the food vendors didn't know. Sam crisscrossed the ten-acre park repeatedly, each time going by the Killer Diller to make sure that Jesse wasn't already there, doing whatever it was that would cause the cars to slip off the rail and crash.

Nothing. There was no sign of Jesse Bartlett.

The wind was unsteady, sometimes tossing debris and trash ahead of itself, sometimes dying away and leaving the grounds in an uneasy stillness. Instinctively, Sam checked the sky for the telltale green tinge that would mean a tornado, but it remained purple and threatening.

People were beginning to look at him oddly as he stood in the middle of the park, next to the carousel, waving his arms in frustration as he spoke to Al. "Where *is* he? Are you sure he's even here? Can't you center on him?"

Al shook his head. "We're not up to capacity yet, Sam, I'm sorry. He's supposed to be here now, but Ziggy can't seem to get a fix on him."

"Well tell him to try harder!"

"We're doing everything we can—there! There he is!"

And he was, coming in the front gate with

a cluster of other people, Aline among them. They started across the park toward the roller coaster, with Aline talking to one older man animatedly, barely acknowledging the greetings of her employees.

"That's the Mayor she's talking to," Al said, consulting the handlink. "And the walking skeleton behind him, that's the Sheriff. She must be showing them around before the ride tomorrow." He cocked a glance at the sky. "She'd better hurry up, or they're going to get wet."

Jesse was trailing along at the rear of the group, his head down, staring at the ground. Mellie and Mike McFarland came out of the office trailer and tagged along, Mike with his hands in his pockets and Mellie scurrying to keep up, a hand through his arm. They came to a stop in a rough semicircle around the operator's station at the Killer Diller.

"We'll gather here about a half hour ahead of time," Aline was saying. "Our own Jesse Bartlett will be at the controls, and—"

Sam didn't stop to listen any more. He grabbed Jesse by the arm and pulled him to one side. The older man looked at him as if he'd lost his mind, and a couple of people from the back of the group around Aline turned to see what the disturbance was.

"Jesse, I know what you're planning to do—"

"What the hell are you talking about? Let go of me, boy. Are you crazy?"

Sam flinched, but hung on. "No, I'm not crazy. I've seen the drawings, I know what you're planning. You can't do it, people are going to die!" He was trying to keep his voice down, not attract the attention of any more people than he had to.

Unfortunately Jesse was under no such constraint. "Dammit, Bob, you let me go!" he yelled. There was a startled silence as everyone turned to look. As Jesse flung "Bob's" arm away, the crowd re-formed around them, Aline and the Mayor and the Sheriff pushing their way forward.

"I saw," Sam said to the crowd, still concentrating on Jesse, "I saw the drawings of the roller coaster—"

"He's seeing things again," the Mayor said to no one in particular.

"Didn't he say somebody was going to die?" one woman asked. "Barry, did he say someone would die?"

"I'm telling you there's going to be an ac—"

"Bob, you stop that right now!" Aline lunged between Sam and Jesse, interrupting before he could finish the phrase. "I told you—"

"He keeps seeing things. It's real strange, how he seems to know things." The Mayor hooked his thumbs through his suspenders, caught a look from his wife, and unhooked them with a guilty shrug. Clearly this was a pattern she had spent a married life, unsuccessfully, to break him of.

"He doesn't know anything," Aline said loudly. "Nothing. He's just a carny. He sees things,

256

he hears things, because he's crazy."

Sam looked at her, saw the pictures of Aline that Bob had kept so carefully, for so long; remembered the welcome in her house; felt the betrayal. And when she caught his look, there was guilt in her eyes, and defiance, and a plea for him to understand.

Jesse had stepped back, become a part of the crowd surrounding him, staring at him. The women, all except Aline, made faces and edged behind the men. The Mayor and the Sheriff exchanged knowing glances, and the Sheriff rested one hand significantly on his holstered gun.

"Al," Sam whispered. "Al, they don't believe me."

"See?" She spun back to her audience, talking fast and loud. "He's talking to himself again! He's not important. Just ignore him, all right? He's not dangerous, he just has some funny ideas. We'll take care of him, won't we, Jesse?"

"Yes we will," Jesse said, from within the crowd. Sam didn't like that neutral tone of voice.

The crowd nodded to one another, satisfied, and remembering their manners, turned back to the ride and Aline.

"Sam, you've got to do something," Al warned, "the odds are going up."

"How can odds of ninety-eight point six go *up*?" Sam said despairingly. "How can I keep it from happening?"

The crowd murmured, uncomfortable. Jesse shook his head, grinning.

Shadows crossed the faces in the crowd, and wind tugged at women's hats and men's thinning hair.

"You've got to stop him, Sam. If the accident happens now, they'll—"

"I know what they'll do," he whispered dryly.

"You've got to keep him from doing it." Even Al was beginning to sweat. "Sam, the only thing that's changing is how many people die, six, seven—"

"Jesse, don't do it. Please. They're going to die—"

Jesse shook his head.

"He doesn't even *care*," Al snarled. "That son of a—Sam, take him out!"

"What?" The suggestion was so unexpected that Sam stopped short. The group was beginning to tighten up, their backs to him.

"Take him *out*, Sam! That's the only way to stop him! Knock him out. That way he won't be able to sabotage it!"

"They'll lock me away." The words were so quiet only Al could hear them.

"They'll lock *Bob* away." Al's answer was merciless, unforgiving. "Not you. You'll Leap. Stop Jesse, and you'll Leap."

"They'll lock Bob away," Sam repeated. This time people heard him. Jesse, responding to a silent plea from Aline, came over to him and took his arm to lead him away.

"You can't save Bob," Al yelled. "You have to save the others! You have to stop Jesse! Sam, you've tried everything else! *Take him out!*"

He could find no other alternative. There was nothing else to do. He could see Bob Watkins reflected in Jesse's eyes, a young man who had made nothing of himself but a carny, lame and weak-handed, a carny who saw things and heard things and knew things that no one else would believe, and he calculated the impact point and pressure and the effect on the audience and on Bob's future and balanced it all against seven lives, and struck.

Jesse doubled over, and slid to the ground without a sound. Sam tried to catch him, without success.

Al nodded decisively. "Okay. Leap."

Sam paused, waiting for the sensation.

Nothing happened.

Then the Mayor's wife screamed, and the group exploded with the pressure of men emerging, imploding upon Sam. In moments he was on the ground next to the unconscious Jesse, and the cadaverous Sheriff—who was considerably stronger than he looked—had slapped handcuffs around his wrists.

"Al?" he yelled. "Al!"

"I'm here, Sam, I'm here." Al was frantically whacking at the handlink, which blinked steadily, unaffected by the blows. "It isn't changing! You didn't hit him hard enough!"

Beside him in the red dirt, Jesse moaned, stirred.

"That does it," the Mayor said grimly. "You lock him up, Kennally. I'll be talking to Judge Grant as soon as we're done here. He's not safe to be around anymore."

Aline knelt over him, holding his head in her hands, ignoring the runs in her stockings, the smears of dirt on her dress. "Bob—"

She shouldn't be ignoring Jesse that way, he thought, and tried to touch her hand.

"You better not be too close, Aline girl." Sheriff Kennally was tugging gently at her, pulling her away.

He couldn't touch her hand. His hands were chained together. Manacled.

And he had failed.

Dry-eyed, he wept.

When he was a teenager, he had discovered the beauty of machines, how they functioned, the movement of gears and ball bearings and blades. For amusement he designed Rube Goldberg-like devices, in which a lit lamp would awaken a parrot which would peck at a dish of marbles which would fall off and trigger an arrow which would burst a balloon which would . . . eventually . . . chop off a chicken's head.

From this he learned the pleasures of violence at a distance.

Machines, so powerful, so elegant, were so vulnerable. And the silly, trusting humans who used them, operated them, drove them without knowing how they worked, were so easily caught by those blades and gears.

It was their own fault, really, every time. If they didn't have the sense to know what they had built, how to make sure it was working properly, then it served them right when the machines failed and caught their tender bodies and crushed them, broke them. It wasn't his fault, it was theirs. They had a responsibility to their machines. They needed to care for them better.

Otherwise anything could happen.

All it would take, for instance, to cause a terrible accident on a roller coaster was to remove the right bolt. And of course, certain other actions, perhaps a trifle more complicated, weakening the scaffolding, disabling the air brakes, a few other things. A very few.

A good safety check would catch most of them.

All his life, it seemed, he had been practicing for this moment. He had spent his life working on machines. This would be his greatest moment, the moment that would fully express his anger, his contempt for the weak people who used machinery without understanding it and tried to blame someone else when they were hurt.

And they would cry, oh, how they would cry and bleed, and all for him. For love of him.

CHAPTER
NINETEEN

If he looked out the window of the jail cell in the direction of Schaeber's Family World, he could see the wall of the Jasmine Public Library. It was painted yellow, faded by sun and weather to a glowing wheaten color. The light reflected from the library window through the bars, onto the floor of the cell, in stripes.

They had led him in, taken the manacles off his hands, and left. By the time the door had clanged shut behind them he was at the window, trying the bars. The building was built new since the Depression, and the bars held.

The Door opened behind him, and he listened for Al's footsteps, knowing he wouldn't hear them. He thought about saying something dry and bitter, or dry and humorous, but he couldn't think of anything to say at all. So he waited, silent, his forehead pressing against the bars.

"Sam, I'm sorry."

It was so inadequate, so sincere, that he couldn't help himself. He laughed. Turning, he caught sight of the look on Al's face, and was sorry. "Al, no, it's—well, it's not okay." He hauled in a deep breath. "But of all the things that won't help now, obsessing about what we should have done instead tops the list."

Al wasn't ready to be forgiven yet. He refused to meet Sam's eyes. "Ziggy says there's a seventy-eight percent chance that—I mean, there's a twenty-two percent chance you're going to get out of here. There's got to be something you can do."

He waited the Observer out, courteously. "Well, whatever it is, the bars are out."

Twenty-two percent. Al was reaching as hard as he could, trying as hard as he could.

Still, twenty-two percent wasn't that bad. Slightly better than one chance in five. He sat on the bunk, shifted to find a place where the mattress wasn't worn to threads, finally lay down, shielding his eyes with one arm.

"You aren't giving up, are you?"

"No." He didn't feel like going into details.

"You have to get out—"

"I know, Al. Why don't you go find out how." For the time being he wanted to be by himself. Since he couldn't come out and say so out loud without hurting the other man's feelings, he simply remained quiet, knowing the message would get through eventually.

It did. After a short while Al gave up, opened the Door and stepped through. Sam listened to the ghostly sound of the Door sliding shut behind the hologram, a sound only he could hear.

Doubtless Al had gone to try to find out more from Ziggy. Sam knew, without knowing how, that Ziggy couldn't help this time. Al and the computer would do the best they could, but in the present day in Jasmine, Oklahoma, Al was only a hologram, and all he could offer was information.

Sam had all the information necessary. He had to put it together, use those much-vaunted brains, solve it himself. Al kept telling him he was a genius. He ought to be able to figure out how to get out, stop Jesse, Leap out of here.

Simple, right? Right.

The fact that deep inside, he was scared to death, was peculiarly irrelevant. He'd been through all that and come out the other side. It was still there, but it didn't matter anymore.

The cell door was locked, no question. The bars were solid. He didn't have any lockpicks on him, and even if he did, he didn't know how to pick locks—now that might be something Al could help with. Al probably knew all about picking locks.

Sure. If he had some bacon, he could have bacon and eggs, if he had some eggs.

So whatever escape there was had to come from outside. He recalled once luring a particularly stupid deputy into a cell, but someone else had been the decoy. And the deputy here was six six and weighed at least two forty. Jasmine was a law-abiding town; he was the only one in the block of four cells. They didn't even get drunks here. Given the size of the local law he could understand why.

Just crazy carnies. So maybe they'd come in and feed him supper, and he could take somebody out that way.

But then they'd have a manhunt. Would they delay the opening for a manhunt? Not Aline Schaeber. He had recognized the look in her eyes, the determination. She wouldn't stop that ride for the Second Coming, not now.

Maybe that was why the number of victims kept changing. Six or seven—if the Sheriff was off looking for an escaped crazy, he wouldn't be riding the roller coaster. He wouldn't die.

Well, he could save one life that way. He had the feeling that one life wouldn't be enough this time. All right, timing was important. Timing was everything.

In Jasmine, Oklahoma, time was slow and languid. The bar-shadows slid across the floor and over the unmoving body of the man lying on the bunk, up the wall to the ceiling, where dark bars and light faded and blended into the late evening, and the crickets came out to sing.

"Bob? Bobby James? I brought you something."
It was Vera, dressed properly in a hat and veil
and prim white gloves, carrying a basket. "That
Martha Jenkins doesn't know cooking from a
gnat's eyebrow, so I brought you some potpie and
plum cobbler." She glared at the deputy until he
meekly opened the door. "This young man tried
to tell me you were dangerous. Nonsense. Stand
up when I'm talking to you, young man. I don't
care if you are in jail, I want you to remember
your manners."

The light from the dangling electric bulb in
the corridor was a harsh glare, and he winced as
he moved his arm and stood stiffly. Vera gazed
for a long moment up into his face and sniffed.
"Dangerous, my foot." She shoved the basket
into his arms. "I want you to eat every bit of
that, do you hear? I won't be having my good
food going to waste. There are people starving
in China."

"Yes, ma'am. Miss Vera—"

"What?" she snapped, pausing at the door.
"You just put the spoon back in the basket when
you're through. They wouldn't let me give you a
knife and fork like a civilized human being, but
I won't let you eat with your fingers. You're not
some animal, that's what I told them."

"Thank you," he said humbly.

Her flintlike gaze softened. "You're a good
boy, Bobby James. You've never hurt a living
soul in your life before, and I'm the first one

267

to say it. You've always told the truth about what you've seen and heard. It isn't your fault if people don't believe you."

"Do you believe me?" he asked quietly.

Vera blinked. "I believe you saw what you say you saw. That's all I know." With that she was gone, leaving the basket behind her on the bunk. The deputy turned the key in the lock and sauntered away, whistling.

He didn't have much of an appetite. He opened the top flap of the linen napkin that covered the basket, and flipped it closed again.

The deputy closed the door to the cell block behind him. He was alone. Not even Al to help him out.

" 'I was always free up here,' " he quoted to the empty air, tapping his forehead. "Up here." He shook the barred door, peering down the corridor between cells to the door the deputy had exited through. "But you never stopped trying, did you, Al?" He paced from one side of the cell to the other. "You didn't sit around and wait— and wait—and wait. . . ."

The twilight outside was swallowed by the dark, and the only light was provided by the bare bulb dangling at the end of the cord. The shadows danced as the bulb moved minutely in the eddying air. Somewhere in the front office a door slammed. A few minutes later the door edged open and a hand fumbled for the light switch, leaving him in darkness. He could hear the sounds of a television set in the front office, with the theme from *The Jackie Gleason Show*, and The Great One saying, "How sweet it is!" A rerun, no doubt, for summer.

He wedged the basket between himself and the wall—no sense in leaving it on the floor for the roaches, Vera would never forgive him—and lay down beside it. "Always free in my mind," he murmured.

And eventually the crickets sang him to sleep.

Sometime past midnight a spring worked loose in the bunk and jabbed him in the ribs. He rolled over, into the picnic basket, and remembered where he was. Circumstances did not seem to have changed appreciably. He went back to sleep. There was nothing more he could do.

Sunday

CHAPTER TWENTY

Bessa woke up before the sun, courtesy of Maxie, purring by her ear. She got up and got herself dressed—she was a big girl—and fed her cat and herself equal helpings of cereal and milk. Then, quietly because her parents were still asleep, she crept out the door. Maxie followed after, and she put her finger to her lips.

"Shhh, Maxie. There's going to be lots and lots of people today. You can't come. You'd get losted."

Maxie plopped his furry bottom down, unconvinced. "Murp?"

"You be quiet, Maxie. You can come later."

Philosophically, Maxie began washing his face, and Bessa shut the door softly behind herself and went skipping down the steps. This was a big day, a wonderful day. There would be lots and lots of people today. Today they would start the roller coaster.

Aline Schaeber too woke in darkness, her stomach churning. She had expected her first thoughts to be of the roller coaster, of the opening; instead she could not shake the memory of Bob, despair and determination on his face, swinging at Jesse. And then lying on the ground, staring up at a circle of faces and pale, so pale, so frightened and desperate.

Jesse was right, he must have gone completely mad. Bob had always been shy, unassuming. He used to shadow her around sometimes when they were children, and she had never once had any reason to feel afraid of him. She still wasn't afraid of him; but she was very much afraid for him.

With a quick breath, she wrenched herself away from the problem of Bob and back to the other event of her life. It was here at last, delayed too long. She spared a quick, sorrowful thought for Karl, who had wanted so much to see his idea come to fruition, to see the people crowd into his amusement park. If there was any justice, he would be looking down from heaven at her today, and smiling. She could see the merry smile, feel the laughter of his eyes. This was her gift to him, her thanks for taking her in and giving her a home and an education and love, and she was sure that somewhere he would receive her gift and know she had succeeded at last. Only a few more hours left, and she would have the best, most popular amusement park in Oklahoma.

Jesse Bartlett ate scrambled eggs for breakfast as he had every Sunday he could remember, steadily chewing and swallowing without tasting. Ruin, that's what they were looking at. Ruin. Loss of everything. Like Dace had lost everything. Maybe he should have let Bob wreck things, day before yesterday. Maybe that would have shown Aline. But it was too late by then, she'd taken out her loan. Damned loan. Damned banks. Nothing would convince her what she was doing was wrong. She needed to keep her head down, collect the money and not try to expand. She was too ambitious, and pride went before a fall. That roller coaster, that was going to be Aline Schaeber's fall.

He washed the last of the eggs down with strong black coffee and stared bleakly out the window toward the amusement park.

Mike McFarland folded his dress shirt quickly and neatly, putting it in exactly the right corner of the battered leather suitcase. The envelope in his suit pocket crackled comfortingly. He already had another job lined up in California, but he didn't expect to need it. A man could get by for a long time on seven thousand dollars, and he had earned

275

every penny of it through honest work. He could spend it through honest play. The job in California was just his excuse to leave quickly. He always found it best to leave quickly. People paid attention to him while he was telling them how to build their amusements, they treated him like an important man. Afterward they had no time for him any more.

They'd have no time for him after the ride opened this time, either. A smile crossed his face. He was glad that he was staying to see it. It really was his greatest achievement, and it really would be beautiful. It always amazed him that people really wanted to ride roller coasters, wanted to scream and be terrified. Well, the Killer Diller would certainly do that. It was unique of its kind, and he was terribly proud of it. He laid his shaving kit and his brushes in beside the shirt, unable to keep the smile off his face. His Killer Diller.

He couldn't wait to see it in action.

The morning sun hit the cell directly, slowly wakening him. For a moment he forgot where he was. Then he remembered all too quickly: hitting Jesse, the sheriff, the manacles, the look on Aline's face.

The deputy came in, clanging a cup against the bars, carrying a plate with a paper napkin carelessly draped over it. "Breakfast, Bobby James," he yodeled. Sam opened one eye, measuring the man. He hadn't shrunk overnight. Sam closed the eye again.

The cell door came open just wide enough to admit the plate. When Sam didn't get up, the deputy lowered it to the floor. "Better move it before the waterbugs get it," the deputy advised. The door slammed shut again.

From the other side of town came the sound of church bells. It was Sunday. Sam wondered suddenly how Aline Schaeber managed to get permission to have her amusement park open on a Sunday, much less have the grand opening of a new ride. He thought there was something about blue laws and the Bible Belt that said people couldn't play on Sunday.

Groaning, he sat up, holding his head in his hands. Out of the corner of his eye he saw the last few legs of a large black cockroach disappear under the paper napkin covering the plate on the floor.

Now if he were some kind of escape artist, he could take a cockroach and the no-doubt-congealed scrambled eggs and manufacture a small nonlethal bomb. Unfortunately he was only a quantum physicist with a picnic basket and no good ideas. He was getting tired of not having any good ideas.

The paper napkin rustled and moved.

"Visitor, Bobby James." It was Vera again, escorted by the deputy. She marched in and glared at the plate on the floor, then at the picnic basket.

"Bobby James Watkins, are you going to *sit* there—" Sam bolted to his feet—"and tell me you didn't eat that supper I spent so much time and effort making for you?"

"I'm sorry, Miss Vera, I just wasn't hungry. I'm sure it was wonderful."

Vera nibbled her withered lips, her gloved fists clenched. "Not hungry? What are you thinking of? You can't afford to be not hungry!" She marched over and snatched up the basket, holding it to herself like a child. "Now you listen to me, Bobby James Watkins. I am going to go home and I am going to fix you a good hearty dinner. And I'm telling you, you are going to eat it. Or you can spend the rest of your days in here eating the kind of food," she snapped her head at the moving napkin, "they provide in places like this. Do you understand me?"

"Yes, ma'am," he said, not understanding at all.

The deputy left the plate behind when he took Vera out again.

He spent the next several hours watching the napkin move. Al didn't show. Two more cockroaches came out from under the bunk and joined the first under the napkin, which twitched even more. He had a quiet wager with himself that the napkin would get walked completely off the plate and down the hall before he could figure out a way to escape this time.

By the shadows and the gnawing in his stomach, it was past noon when Vera showed up

278

again, looking a trifle disheveled. "It's late," she told him. "Past one o'clock. You'd better eat up."

"I sure will," he said gratefully. "Thanks, Miss Vera."

As he reached for the basket she pulled it away. "You promise me you'll eat everything you can," she said. "You promise me that, boy. I'm not going to all this trouble on your account not to have my efforts appreciated, you hear?"

"Yes, ma'am," he agreed. Her gaze searched his, and she handed him the basket as if she were entrusting it to him. An idea blossomed in the back of his mind as he accepted the basket she was so eager that he have.

The deputy had another plate in his hand, and he grinned as he looked from the basket to the plate. "Well, I think you got the better of it this time, Bobby James."

"I think I did," Sam said, watching the woman standing before him. "I think I got it better than I knew."

A gleam of relief shone in the tired eyes. "And about time," Vera snapped, and marched away. The guard, shaking his head at the vagaries of old women, followed her.

Sam sat down on the bunk and unfolded the linen napkin, fold by fold. It was there, buried between the blueberry muffin and the potpie. If he'd had a little more interest in things, or a little more appetite, he could have used it last night. Or a little more faith. Whatever.

It was past one o'clock—past one-thirty, according to the clock chimes from the town square. He had to get moving.

"Deputy," he yelled through a mouthful of muffin. There was no question Vera's baking was miles better than her lemonade.

The only question was, where did Vera Schaeber find herself an old-fashioned cosh?

CHAPTER
TWENTY-ONE

There was a bigger crowd at Schaeber's than he had ever seen, milling and shouting above the music, and more coming in all the time. The teenage boy taking admissions was overwhelmed. He was able to slip in without attracting attention and follow the torrent of people all heading to the west end of the park.

Jugglers and mimes threaded through the crowd, which grew even thicker the closer he got to the Killer Diller. He could almost believe the park would pull itself out of its financial hole—until he reminded himself of what would happen unless he succeeded. He ducked out of sight of Miguel and some other vendors and pressed on.

There they were, gathered around the operator's station. Aline and the Mayor were already seated in the first car, the Mayor looking pale and holding onto the safety bar even though the cars hadn't started moving yet. Aline looked excited, happy, incongruous in white gloves and hat, very much the Oklahoma small-town lady. Behind them others were getting in, one by one. Jesse stood by the operator's stand, ready to throw the lever to start the cars moving. The crowd was so dense that children were being carried on the shoulders of their fathers to see the ride better.

Sam, still on the periphery, stepped on a rock and his leg turned under him. He struggled to his feet and kept going. The people around him moved, not enough to let him through, just enough to let him see.

They were all in the cars now, Aline and the Mayor, the banker's wife and McFarland and all the others, looking as if they wondered what on earth normal sane adult human beings were doing on a child's ride—one they would never let their children on. But it was exciting. Everyone thought it was exciting. They were all ready to go wherever the ride would take them. All the people had bought tickets to come and see. Many had already bought tickets for their turn on the ride, once the opening ride was done, and more were lined up, clamoring to give their money. Aline was red-cheeked and smiling, her eyes shining.

And they saw, as Sam saw, Mike McFarland get up out of his seat and tap Aline on the shoulder, gesture toward Jesse, poised to start the ride and send the cars through the big pink ribbon for the Grand Opening. They saw him speak to her with insistence and urgency.

They saw Aline call out to Jesse Bartlett, the general manager of the park, the trusted and valued friend and partner and employee of Karl Schaeber and now of Aline herself, and wave him into the seat McFarland had so generously vacated.

They saw Jesse take McFarland's place, confused and reluctant, and Mike McFarland stand with one hand on the operating lever and the other hand in his pocket, a smile on his face. They saw, and Sam saw, and Sam knew. It was not Jesse, whose dreams were too small to contain a roller coaster, who would cause the wreck.

It was McFarland, who was laughing and fingering a bolt in his pocket. A bolt to hold a guide rail securely against the wooden center beam of the track. He could see it. He could see it—

"McFarland!" he shouted. "Stop!"

And McFarland turned around and saw Bobby James Watkins, the crazy, the cripple, coming toward him, saw the knowledge in his eyes, and he laughed again, pulling a heavy steel bolt from his pocket as Sam lunged.

The cars began to move. Sam yanked at the brake switch, and the audience, not yet understanding that there was something wrong, gasped. The passengers in the cars looked back and at each other, and some of the men tried to get to their feet and were pulled back into their seats by nervous companions.

Nothing happened. Sam spun, staggered on his bad leg, and McFarland stepped back to give him room, still laughing, waving the bolt in front of him to taunt him. Sam threw himself against the emergency-brake crash bar and felt it give loosely under his hands. The cars kept moving, building up their slow momentum, climbing up the hill to the crown, where all the potential energy would be loosed at almost sixty miles an hour.

"What's the matter, Bobby? You got a problem here?"

In the cars, the Mayor and the Sheriff and their wives and all the other passengers were craning their necks to see what was going on behind them. It served to distract them from the steep climb to the seventy-foot crown of the first hill. Then they looked down and saw the earth pulling away from them, and began to understand that something was wrong, very wrong.

It would take less than two minutes to reach the top of the crown. Sam glared wildly upward, the equations spinning through his head without conscious calculation. The swaying of the wooden structure under the weight of cars and passengers would jar the unbolted guide rail out of alignment with the guide rail of the next section. And then the lead wheel would reach the end of the loose rail and with nothing to hold them to the track, the cars would plummet to the ground. The top brake, positioned to slow the cars just before they reached the top to make sure they didn't rocket over the edge, was useless. There was nothing that could be done, unless the rail could be fixed in place.

Which required the bolt.

Sam whipped around, moving faster than he had ever moved, and snatched. He was almost startled to feel the metal weight in his hand. McFarland ceased laughing and yelped in dismay. "Hey! No! What are you doing?"

Without further threat to McFarland, Sam raced up the walkboard, not bothering to answer. The chain was slow, and he passed the cars, feeling the wood under his feet lurch, grabbing at the handrail. When the slope got too steep, he lunged for the laddering of the scaffold. He was halfway to the top when McFarland realized what he had in mind and came after him.

His arm—Bob Watkins' arm—was weak. It ached fiercely as he pulled himself upward. He had almost reached the top when the pursuing McFarland grabbed his ankle and tried to pull him loose. For a dizzying moment he was looking, not at the railing in front of his nose, but down at the tops of the trees that shaded the town of Jasmine, down at the still gray waters of Milsom's Pond.

"Sam!" It was Al, floating in the air beside him.

The cars were coming closer. He could see the faces of the passengers clearly, as clearly as they could see him. Time seemed to stretch and slow.

285

He could see their mouths moving, but couldn't hear the voices.

Beside him, Al was shouting, holding up the handlink. He couldn't stop to pay attention.

Beneath him the scaffold swayed and creaked, and one of the ladder supports fell away. His foot—Bob's weak foot—slid, caught on something. McFarland snatched at his leg again, and in doing so shoved it back onto a crossbeam. Sam looked down to identify the other man's location, and swallowed a rush of nausea as he saw past him and down through the cage of scaffolding seventy feet to the ground.

"You can't do it!" McFarland screamed. "You can't!" Sabotaged ladder steps had fallen away beneath him, too, unable to stand the passage of two men while the cars were shaking the ride as well, and he was clinging to a support beam with one arm and snatching with the other.

"Sam, he's crazy! He's responsible for all the accidents! He's been hinking up machinery everywhere he goes!"

"Now you tell me," Sam said between his teeth, steadying himself against the beam and holding onto the safety rope. He would have to stretch full length on the track to reach the center rail. The side rails and the top brake were all missing, raw wood showing where they had been torn out as recently as the night before, perhaps even when he was fighting with Jesse. There was nothing to hold the cars in place. They would shoot over the edge and into the

286

earth, taking seven people with them.

The cars were coming closer. His fingertips brushed the end of the guide rail, the open bolt hole. The metal was burning hot from the mid-day sun. Grunting, he transferred the bolt from one hand to the other.

"Sam, he's one of those wackos, psychotics, he likes to see people get hurt—"

"You can't stop it!" McFarland wailed. "Don't stop it! It's mine!"

Some of the passengers realized what he was doing as he lay full out on the track, reaching for the metal bar. They shrieked uselessly. The peo-ple below, unable to understand what was going on, able only to see the two men clambering on the creaking beams and the ride advancing on them both, cheered lustily.

Ignoring them all, Sam wedged the bolt into the hole in the rail. It wouldn't go through; the connecting piece had edged out of alignment, and the rail was beginning to shift. He levered himself up to get a better grip, and McFarland grasped the hem of his jeans. The lower part of his body swung free, flailing for purchase. Someone in the approaching cars screamed again. Some-one on the ground screamed louder. Somehow he managed to catch hold of something with his toes.

Iron fingers wrapped themselves around Bob Watkins' leg, bit into the withered muscles, hauled the leg free. Sam swayed and rolled, with no safety line to hang onto, and grabbed the track beam by one hand, gasping as a splinter jabbed deep, making his palm slippery with sweat and blood. The track shuddered under him. McFarland came level with his prone body, shoved with all his strength. The cars were too close.

"Sam!" Al yowled.

For a moment that lasted longer than any moment he could ever remember, he found himself twisted around, staring into the eyes of McFarland and madness. He clung for his life to the support beam, and McFarland leaned into him, pushing, his breath warm and shocking against Sam's face. Sam jerked back, away, and almost slid free.

And McFarland, expecting resistance and finding none, lost his precarious balance. In a split second the madness was gone, replaced by terror, and he reached for Sam again, not to push him away, but for balance, for support, for help; and Sam, unthinking, reached out automatically, only to feel the other man's fingers slide uselessly past his as McFarland fell, screaming until his body collided with the first structural beam. The impact nearly sent Sam hurtling after him. It jolted the bolt free, sending it spinning to the earth. The first car had reached the sabotaged section. Aline and the Mayor could see the guide rail shifting. So could Sam.

As if in slow motion, he reached out, yanked the madly vibrating metal back in place, and jerked his hand away.

The cars shot by, scant inches from his sleeve, still on the track.

"I don't *know* why you haven't Leaped, Sam," Al fretted. "You did what you were supposed to do. They all saw what happened, and nobody thinks Bob is responsible for the problems with the ride. They're still finding things going wrong, by the way. The way McFarland designed it, it was a wonder it held together as long as it did."

"Right," Sam said abstractedly, rearranging the prizes in the duck shoot booth.

"And there's absolutely *no* danger of Bob being sent away to an asylum.

"But Aline uses the money she was going to pay McFarland to redesign the coaster safely, and it's a big success. Seems people think it's even more thrilling to ride. They don't call it Killer Diller anymore, though," he added as an afterthought.

"That's good." A blue stuffed elephant was obscured by a collection of pink chickens. Sam moved it up to a hook depending from the ceiling, where it revolved peacefully, trunk waving to the passersby. The booth was in perfect shape now, air rifles all lined up neatly, ducks in a row.

" 'That's good'? That's all you can say? 'That's good'?" Al was looking considerably more chipper this Sunday evening. His electric-blue suit fairly sparkled in the lights from the Imaging

Chamber. "Sam, what's wrong? You've been awfully quiet lately."

Sam shrugged. "Got something else to take care of, I guess," he said. "Has to be, right? Otherwise I'd have Leaped." He never looked in the direction of the roller coaster.

Around the booth, the lights of the amusement park were springing into being against the Oklahoma twilight. The music from the calliope started, stopped, began again, setting the rhythm for the dancing carousel figures. Children were screaming with pleasure, laughing, shouting, running. Sam crouched under the bench and plugged in his own lights. Behind him, the ducks began their slow advance through the painted cardboard waves, dropping out of sight at one end of the booth and popping up again at the other.

"Sam, why won't you talk to me?" Al said plaintively.

"I'm not finished yet," he said, looking around the booth. Everything was in place. He placed his hands flat on the shooting bench and leaned over, looking both ways; Al scooted out of his line of vision, still confused.

"Bob?" It was Aline. She was still pale, but her hair was perfectly in place, her lipstick unsmudged, her gloves spotless. She was the image of a lady. Aunt Vera would have been proud of her. Aunt Vera, hovering behind her, obviously was. She was beaming impartially at them both.

On the other end of the counter, Maxie the cat leaped up, purring.

"Aline," Sam acknowledged. He looked over the counter. "Bessa." He nodded again to Aline, raised the partition, and lifted the little girl to sit on the bench on the inside of the booth.

Aline looked nervously at the little girl, decided not to worry about her. Vera nudged her imperatively. "All right! All right."

"Bob, I came to apologize. I am so sorry for what I said. What I did. I was so wrong. I didn't mean it. I was—well, I was scared."

"I know." He had one arm around Bessa, steadying her. The cat rubbed his head against Sam's shoulder, rumbling loudly.

Vera nudged Aline again. Aline glared at her aunt and went on, "You really did see—last Wednesday, you really did see something, didn't you? You saw Mike drop the bolt. That's what you were saying."

Sam shrugged, deprecating. "I guess so." Bessa was fingering a blue bunny rabbit with one hand, chewing the fingers of the other. He gently took her hand out of her mouth. "Remember," he murmured. "Big girls don't."

Aline took a deep breath, steeling herself. "Will you forgive me?"

His eyes met hers, and he smiled. "I'll forgive you."

"Oh, good, Sam, that must be it. Now you'll Leap." Al read the handlink with startled enthusiasm. "Hey, it's a whole new future. Bob and

Aline don't get married, but—well, not to each other, but they get married. Bob goes into a repair shop business with Jesse, and they do okay, too."

"I'm not quite through yet, though," Sam said, to both Aline and Al. Both of them looked up, surprised.

"Bessa, what do you want more than anything?" he said to the little girl.

Her blue eyes shifted from his face to the rabbit and back again, eloquent.

"More than anything?"

She nodded.

Sam picked up one of the air rifles, sighted carefully, and fired, once, twice, three times, and three ducks in a row fell down, *clang, clang, clang*.

"Here you are," he said, handing her the blue bunny.

Then he looked Aline square in the eye. "You see, sometimes a heart's desire is a lot more simple than you think it is."

Maxie, sitting next to the ecstatic Bessa, chirped agreement, and put out one snow-white paw as if dubbing him noble, or calling for his attention, or asking for food.

The tiny pinpricks of the cat's claws were the last thing he felt as he Leaped.

EPILOGUE

He floated again in the blue-white light, without weight, without sensation, waiting for the Voice. After a while it came again.

"Dr. Beckett." It was different this time, higher, but it was the same voice. He would know that voice anywhere, forever.

"Here I am." Wherever 'here' was. It was not earth and it was not heaven. It was his own mind, he thought. This was what his own mind was like, from the inside. This is what time itself was like, from the inside.

But the voice was outside, part of him and not part of him. He didn't understand that part yet. He would have to think about it—float in the light and think.

I think, therefore I am. *I still am.*

"You did well at the last. You didn't let your fears overcome you. That was very good."

He grasped at hope. "Does that mean I can go home?"

The Voice paused, considering, and he could feel the hope building. But the pause went on too long as he floated timelessly in sometime, no time, and hope slipped away. And the voice said, regretfully, "No. Not yet."

"Someday?" he asked, hope battling disappointment.

"Someday," the Voice promised. "Someday."

And then, "Are you ready, Dr. Beckett?"

And he Leaped.